DETROIT PUBLIC LIBRARY

W9-BXD-978

The *21* Lives *of*
Lisette Donavan

shelved under
"Williams"

Popular Library
Detroit Public Library
5201 Woodward Ave.
Detroit, MI 48202

JUN - - 2012

PL

2   *Tallahassee Authors Network*

Detroit, MI 48202

The *21* Lives *of* Lisette Donavan

Compiled by: Barbara Joe Williams

Amani Publishing, llc

Barbara Joe Williams

Tallahassee, FL

This book is a work of fiction. Any names, characters, places, and incidents are either the product of the author's imagination or used fictitiously. Any resemblance to actual persons, living or dead, or to actual events or locales is entirely coincidental.

Copyright © 2012 Compiled by: Barbara Joe Williams

Individual stories are copyrighted by the authors

All rights reserved. No part of this book may be reproduced in any form without the expressed written permission of the publisher, except by a reviewer.

Amani Publishing, LLC
P. O. Box 12045
Tallahassee, FL 32317
(850) 264-3341

A company based on faith, hope, and love

Visit our website at: **www.barbarajoewilliams.com**

Email us at: **amanipublishing@aol.com**

ISBN: 9780983366614
LCCN: 2012905806

Cover photo courtesy of: Bigstockphoto.com
Cover creation by: Diane Bass

History of the Tallahassee Authors Network

The Tallahassee Authors Network (TAN) was founded in September 2008 by two local authors, Marilynn Griffith and Barbara Joe Williams. The network was formed as a means to bring all locally published authors, aspiring writers, and avid readers together in one venue. Since the beginning, we've met on a bi-monthly basis at one of the local libraries.

We occasionally have guest speakers, such as attorneys, editors, graphic artists, and photographers, who visit our meetings. However, our main mission is to provide a supportive environment where new and seasoned authors can network with readers and learn from each other's unique experiences. We also discuss the latest books, publishing trends, marketing ideas, literary events, and everything related to reading, writing, and publishing.

Many of our authors are self-published or independent publishers, but we also have some traditionally published authors in our group. We're open to supporters from all ethnic backgrounds and encourage all genres of writers to attend our general meetings on a regular basis.

We also have a group Facebook page, which is open to authors all over the world. Although these authors cannot attend our bi-monthly sessions, they are encouraged to participate in our annual TAN Showcase.

Letter to the Reader

Dear Reader,

Thank you for purchasing a ticket to journey with us through the twenty-one lives of Lisette Donavan, presented by members of the Tallahassee Authors Network. The idea behind this project was born from a writing workshop.

During the course of the writing workshop, we collectively created a character profile beginning with a female by the name of Lisette Donavan. After completing the basic profile, we were given five-minutes to write our own individual stories surrounding this one main character.

At the end of the session, each participant was invited to share their story with the group. Everyone was amazed at the various stories that were all based on one profile, and the amount of talented writers in the room.

After the meeting, it was suggested that we expand our writings into short stories that we could publish into an anthology. And since I'm a publisher, I decided to accept the challenge.

Now six-months later, I'm delighted to present our collective work to you. Please sit back, relax, and enjoy the many characteristics of Lisette Donavan. And when you're done, you'll be invited to provide feedback to individual authors and vote on your favorite story via an online survey site.

Sincerely,

Barbara Joe Williams, publisher

Table of Contents

1. *Full Circle* ©Shantae Charles
2. *A Wicked Twist of Fate* ©Angela Y. Hodge
3. *There Are No Mountains* ©John McPhaul
4. *Empty Pockets* ©Laurina Osborne
5. *You Can Never Leave* ©Melinda Michelle
6. *Last Date with Elijah* ©Thomas R. Wilson
7. *Gettin' My Happy* ©Xavier D. Woods
8. *Wrong Turns* ©Irma Clark
9. *Country Girl, City Girl, Bad Girl* ©Jane Ann Keil-Stevens
10. *Family Ties* ©Shay Shoats
11. *A Voice of MY Own* ©Anita L. Gray
12. *In Due Time* ©Erica Belcher
13. *Accomplice* ©Sylvia Livingston
14. *I Want My Piece* ©Tremayne Moore
15. *Maid to Survive* ©Karen Randolph
16. *Lissy Transforming* ©Angelia Vernon Menchan
17. *Lisette Donavan's American Dream* ©Cheryl B. Williams
18. *Diary of a Sneaky Woman* ©Michael Beckford
19. *The Snake* ©Kenneth E. Taite
20. *Double D Death* ©Felicia S.W. Thomas
21. *You Don't Even Know My Name* ©Barbara Joe Williams

Dedication

This book is dedicated to all the aspiring authors around the world. We hope that you will see this book as an inspiration to keep writing and pushing towards your publishing goals.

-Tallahassee Authors Network-

1.

Full Circle

Shantae Charles

Thirty days. God, I don't think I can take another day of this.

Lisette rubbed her eyes, yawned, and stretched her arms wide in an effort to ready her body for another round of work. At twenty-eight, it wasn't what she'd imagined herself doing, but with an insider trading charge against her, her career in stock exchange was pretty much down the toilet. It didn't matter that, Thad, her oh-so-false fiancé had been the one exchanging information. He had thrown her under the bus in his plea for a lighter sentence.

What hurt the most wasn't the accusation, but the look of disappointment in her family's eyes during the trial. As the oldest and the first to go to college on full scholarship, her twin siblings, Jade and Jaden, had looked to her with awe and admiration. That admiration had turned to confusion and disillusionment as they witnessed their sister being taken away. Her bright orange jumpsuit would forever color their memories of her. Lisette had gone from being the darling of Wall Street to the laughingstock. She'd been up for a promotion when things had gone awry. Her colleagues had chosen to remain silent for fear of being incriminated amidst all of the "white collar" crackdowns.

Lisette flung the covers off and rolled out of bed. She glanced around her sparse surroundings: alarm clock, one solitary photo of her family at her graduation, and her portfolio of artwork and photography during her twelve months behind bars. She had rediscovered her love for drawing and painting. Thad had discouraged her hobby as he had called it, as unnecessary. It was the one thing Lisette had given up to fit into his world. Funny, how her passion had returned so naturally as if she'd never stopped creating. When she was on break at the hotel, she carried a mini-sketch pad to jot down images she would later turn into full blown pieces. This one-room, hole-in-the-wall had been all she could afford at the moment. She had stayed with her parents for a year after her release to save up money, but after the last blow-up with her father, she had decided it was time to strike out again on her own. She dressed quickly, but efficiently, her housekeeping uniform pressed to perfection, and slipped her small sketchbook into her pocket. She looked at herself in the mirror, her olive skin, sprinkled with light freckles, her naturally curly hair matching the spring in her step. As she closed her hazel eyes, she prayed. *This time, I'm doing this for me and me alone. Whatever the future holds, I'm going to face it with confidence in myself. This is not the end. This is only the beginning.*

December 31, Noon
"Ms. Donavan, may I have a word with you?"

Lisette looked up from the paper she had been engrossed in. Gerard, her floor manager, spoke to her from the door of the break room.

Lisette put her paper down, giving him her full attention. At well over six feet, with wide shoulders, and a genuine smile for everyone, Gerard was both friendly, yet imposing at the same time. He had been more than generous, allowing her to work overtime and double shifts throughout the holidays so that she could put away extra money. Though friendly, he managed to keep a professional distance, always using her last name to address her.

"Here?"

Gerard looked behind him, and then came to sit directly across from her. "I wanted to give you a heads up, but in a few minutes, our hotel manager is going to request you for a meeting."

Lisette tried not to swallow loudly as she took in the information. "Any idea why?"

Gerard ran his hands nervously through his blonde hair. "Well, apparently, you left something in one of the rooms you were cleaning and the guest wanted to return it to you."

Lisette stilled at his words. *My sketchbook.* She had recently been flipping through her sketchbooks and realized one was missing. *It must have slipped out when I was cleaning.* She had only been assigned one room last week due to the client's extended stay. It was a huge "no-no" to bring anything to the rooms when cleaning. She remembered that she hadn't had time to put it in her locker before reporting for her room assignment. *Well, here goes this job.* She had only been there thirty days, and already it seemed she was going to be axed.

"I think I know what it was. I'm so sorry; I honestly didn't mean to take it up there." She looked at him, a silent plea in her eyes. "Whatever I need to do, apologize, clean toilets, take a difficult group, I'll do it. I just can't lose this job," she told Gerard.

Gerard looked at her, sympathy emanating from his ice-blue gaze. "Look, I'm not even sure you're in trouble. I just didn't want you to be caught off guard. You're one of our best workers, and that's saying a lot, you being new to the staff and all." He placed his hand over hers in comfort. "I'll put in a good word for you, so don't panic, okay?"

No sooner than Gerard had reassured her, another co-worker entered the break room. "Ms. Donavan, our hotel manager would like to see you."

Lisette entered the room confidently after being urged to enter, though inwardly she was shaking.

The nameplate, nearly taking up the entire front of her desk, and ornately engraved, read: Daria Foster. She hadn't expected a petite, porcelain-skinned woman. Her strawberry blonde bob framed her face, her features delicate yet stern at the same time. Lisette could tell this woman meant business.

"Have a seat, Ms. Donavan."

The hotel manager had yet to look up at her.

Lisette helped herself to a seat in front of the desk, folding her hands neatly in her lap and waited for the axe to fall. After a few more minutes of interminable silence, she was startled as Daria slapped the folder she had been reviewing down on her desk.

She clasped her hands together thoughtfully, and leaned forward, piercing Lisette with her arctic blue eyes. "Why are you here?"

Lisette straightened up at the question. "I was told to . . ."

Ms. Arctic held up her hand to stop her. "No, why are you *here*?" She spread her hands around the environment. She held up the folder from earlier. "This is your employee file." She tossed it aside once more. "Which, by the way, is a revelation in itself; you hold a Bachelors in Political Science, with a minor in Finance and a Masters in Business Administration. What are you doing cleaning rooms?"

"I have a criminal record because my fiancé decided to steal trading information from the company I was working for. Logically, I was implicated. My degrees meant nothing at this point. So, I'm starting over, trying to save some money, and deciding what I want to do with the rest of my life," Lisette summarized. If she was going to be fired, she may as well put it all out there and be done with it.

"*Have* you decided yet, what you want to do with the rest of your life?" Daria asked.

Lisette shook her head. "I've rediscovered my passions, but no, I haven't decided yet."

"Maybe I can help you decide," said a voice from behind Lisette.

She turned to see a gentleman standing by the window. His accent and thin wiry frame complemented his slightly unkempt hair. His wire-rimmed glasses framed kind eyes the color of brandy. She lowered her head in embarrassment, realizing he had been there the entire time. He came to sit next to Lisette, extending what she was certain was her small sketchbook. She took it from him, politely thanking him.

Daria's tone seemed to change then. "Ms. Donavan, this is one of our most valued guests and also a personal friend of mine, Easton Dubois. Easton, this is Lisette Donavan, the young lady who left the sketch book in your space."

Easton smiled then and extended his hand to Lisette. "It's a pleasure to meet you, Ms. Donavan."

Lisette shook his hand nonplussed. "I'm so sorry. I usually put my sketchbook in my locker, and I must have been in a rush, sir."

Easton waved off the explanation. "No need to apologize, really. I was just fascinated by the sketches, and figured you'd want them. But, more than that, I wanted to meet the artist," he explained. "So, tell me, do you only work in your sketchbook?"

Lisette looked to Daria, who gave her the nod to continue. "Well, I generally carry the sketchbook around and as images come to mind, I jot them down. Then I work in acrylic and on canvas to expand the images into full blown paintings."

Easton looked at Daria, then back to Lisette. "I know this may sound strange, but if you are willing, I'd like to take a look at your pieces. I am an art dealer and curator of a small gallery near Times Square. I've got several buyers who may be interested in your work. I did take your sketches around to a few of them and their interest demanded that I find you. To hear that you've actually got some pieces ready is a great boon." He chuckled. "What do you think about having a private showing? I've already got one scheduled for tonight. All you need do is show up with say, three pieces. If we get a bite, then we could work on setting you up with some studio space and give you an opportunity to create around twenty-five pieces for a larger showing. What do you think?"

Lisette's mind was reeling with the possibilities. "Sir, are you saying you'd like to sponsor me as an artist?"

Easton laughed at her comical expression. "Yes, I would. Your work is very Avant-garde and fresh. We've had some submittals recently and they've been the standard, so we were looking for someone who could shake up the art world. I think you, Ms. Donavan, could do that." He handed her his card.

Before Lisette could protest, he went on. "I'm well aware of how hard it is to combat a bad past and move forward. But this was no coincidence, that I, of all people, should find your sketchbook. The offer to come tonight still stands. The showing starts at 11 P.M., the reception at 10 P.M. Just call the number and leave your address. My chauffer will pick you up along with your pieces."

Lisette pondered his words.

"Well, Ms. Donavan, the choice is up to you. Easton, don't badger the girl. She does have to get back to work. What time does your shift end?" Daria asked.

Lisette looked at her watch. "It ends at eight."

"Perfect. Can we expect to *see* you tonight, at least?" Daria asked.

Lisette felt a calm settle over her. "Yes." She took the notepad offered and scribbled her address.

December 31, 11:00 pm

Lisette couldn't believe she was living in the same day. Just this morning she had been vacuuming and thinking to herself that life had to be more than folding sheets, flipping pillows, and picking lint off bathrobes. Now, as she held her glass of sparkling cider and took in the other works of art, she couldn't believe that her work was being displayed alongside some of the hottest contemporary artists in New York City. *God, you are incredible.*

As she turned, she walked right into a solid chest and recognized the scent before she even looked up.

"Hello, Thad." Lisette spoke, carefully controlling her tone. She refused to let him think he still mattered.

He looked completely surprised. *And well he should be.* Their engagement had ended nearly three years ago now and they hadn't spoken to each other since the trial. She had heard through her parents that he was working at a law firm as a clerk. Her family had since stopped mentioning him once they realized how much anguish it was causing her. To see him now, Lisette felt . . . nothing. And that felt great.

"Lisette! What . . . what are you doing here?"

"What better place to be, among one of my passions?"

Thad seemed to have a mental recollection then. "That's right; you were into the artsy stuff."

"Thad, take a look at this piece. We've got to have it." A woman, no older than twenty-five, sidled up beside him. Blonde, blue-eyed, rail thin; *And nothing like me.*

"Lisette, this is Nora, my fiancée," Thad rambled off quickly, his cheeks flushed with obvious embarrassment.

Nora looked between the two of them, her bubbly personality spilling over and mingling with the wine she had obviously been drinking. "Hi, honey, come, let's buy it before it's gone." She tugged Thad along.

Thad shrugged his shoulders in a gesture of helplessness. "I'll see you around, Lissy," he said, allowing his fiancé to pull him across the gallery. *Now, that was awkward.*

Lisette waved him bye, and smiled, knowing that she would probably never see Thad again after tonight, but by the looks of things, one of her pieces would be hanging in his home. *Funny how things come full circle,* she thought to herself.

Daria and Easton strolled over to her.

"You look fabulous, Lisette, and so in your element." Daria nodded approvingly at her choice of a little black dress with her Jimmy Choos from her former life.

Easton seemed like he couldn't hold in his news one second longer. "You'll be happy to know we've sold all three of your pieces. One we almost had a fight over. Everyone wants to meet you after the showing. I want you to know that all the proceeds for your pieces tonight go to you."

Lisette stood mouth agape. "Mr. Dubois, you don't have to do that. You took a chance on me, after all. You didn't know what I was bringing tonight," Lisette reasoned.

"We'll talk contracts and commission tomorrow if you're up to having New Year's Brunch," Easton suggested, handing her a check.

Lisette looked down at the check and her knees buckled. *Forty thousand dollars for three pieces?*

Easton placed his hand gently on her shoulder. "Don't be surprised, Lisette. Your work is stunning. This was a private showing to people who understand the market value of an unknown female artist who can potentially rock the art world.

Don't underestimate your gift. As for the amount, consider it an investment. I believe you haven't even begun to see what you can create, provided with the right environment."

Lisette had been walking in a measure of confidence, but now, she knew she needed more than that. She needed her faith to be in God, not just her ability. Mr. Dubois would be counting on her to bring her A-game to the table.

"New Year's Brunch sounds great, Mr. Dubois." Lisette shook his hand, staring into his kind eyes. "Thank you for giving me this opportunity. With God's help, I won't disappoint you."

Daria gave her a hug then. "Lisette, you have so much potential. Live up to it, and don't look back." She smiled.

As they walked away, Lisette tucked the check into her clutch bag, marveling to herself at how one's life could so dramatically alter when trusting God. Just then, Daria turned around.

"Oh, and Lisette?"

Lisette stirred from her musings. "Yes?"

Daria chuckled then. "One more thing I forgot to mention: You're fired."

Lisette couldn't help but laugh, for at that seemingly divine moment, the clock struck midnight.

1. Full Circle, Shantae Charles,
    shantaecharles333@gmail.com

2.

A Wicked Twist of Fate

Angela Y. Hodge

Lisette Donavan was sitting at the airport waiting on a cab to take her to her new apartment in New York City. She was tired and frustrated because she had lost out on yet another job opportunity to be a project manager. How long would she have to pay for the mistakes of her youth? She comforted herself by thinking this wasn't the job she truly wanted anyway. Her cell phone rang, startling her from her thoughts. "Hello." It was Nikki, her sister.

"Hey, you have to come home. Matt has been in a bad accident!" Lisette was speechless for a moment, thinking about her older brother.

"Okay, I will book the next flight out. Is Mom okay?"

"Yeah, she's fine. Get here as soon as you can."

Lisette got in line to purchase a plane ticket for her emergency flight back home to Daytona Beach, Florida. Two hours later, she was boarding and looking for her seat. She was lucky to get a straight flight. She would be home in less than two hours. As she was waiting for takeoff, she opened her window cover and looked out at the clouds. Tears began rolling down her cheeks. A tall, brown-skinned flight attendant with blond hair walked up to her. "Excuse me, ma'am. Is everything okay?" Lisette continued to look out of her window. "My name is Kieta. Can I get anything for you?"

"No, I'm okay."

Kieta turned and walked away, shaking her head when a thought occurred to her. "Nah, that can't be. It can't be. It's been ten years since I last saw her." A ton of old memories began to flood Kieta's mind. Her palms became sweaty, and sweat began to stream down her back. Robert, another flight attendant, approached her.

"Girl, what is wrong with you?"

She shook her head.

"Well, you don't look so good, but you have to come and see this woman. She is hot! She is definitely the woman of my dreams."

Keita was unconvinced. "You are always trying to meet somebody, and according to you, everybody is hot."

Robert took her hand. "Just come on and let me show you." As they headed back down the aisle, Robert whispered, "There she is. She's sitting on the ninety-seventh row in Seat C."

"No, no, no, you can't talk to her." Kieta exclaimed.

Confused, Robert asked, "Why not?"

"Just because, okay?"

"Do you know her?"

"I think so, but that can't be her. It just can't be."

"Well, where do you know her from?" Robert asked.

Kieta paused and thought back to a tragic accident that happened ten years ago. She ignored Robert's probing questions.

Oblivious that she was the topic of their conversation, Lisette began to pray. "Lord, give me the strength to make it. Watch over my brother, Matt, and keep him safe, in Jesus' name, Amen."

Robert approached Lisette. "Hi, how are you? My name is Robert. I just had to tell you that you look nice today."

Before Lisette could respond, she was interrupted by the Captain's voice over the intercom. "Will everyone please be seated and buckle up. We have an emergency landing at Norfolk International Airport. Let me assure you not to panic. Everything is under control."

Lisette began to pray, "Lord, please watch over us. I pray that we land safely. Forgive me for all of my sins. In Jesus' name, Amen!"

The plane landed in Norfolk. As they were slowly moving down the runway, Lisette called her sister back.

"Lisette," Nikki said. "Where are you?"

"I am still on the plane. We just had an emergency landing at the Norfolk International Airport. The captain stated that everything was under control, but we may have a small delay. How is Matt?"

"He is now in stable condition. The EMT stated that on their way to the hospital, Matt was asking for you. He said he had something very important to tell you. Do you know what he is talking about?"

"No."

"Well, you'd better get here as soon as possible."

The plane was at a standstill. Kieta walked back over to Lisette. "Are you feeling better?" Kieta asked "You seemed very upset earlier."

Lisette was so desperate to talk to someone she blurted out, "I got a call stating my brother, Matt, was in a bad accident. So I'm heading back home to see him. Now, my sister just told me that he's asking for me."

"I'm sorry to hear that. I hope everything works out for you."

"Thank you! You look familiar. Do I know you from somewhere?" Lisette asked.

Keita shook her head.

Lisette continued. "Your voice sounds like a girl I knew. Do you know a Charlotte Donaldson?"

"No," Keita lied.

Lisette was determined. "Umm, how long have you been working for this airline?"

"Five years. I love traveling, meeting new people, and going to different states."

Something in her gut told Lisette she knew this woman. "Hey, have you ever lived in the Daytona Beach area?"

"No," Keita lied again.

Keita wanted some answers of her own, so she began asking questions. "What kind of work do you do? Maybe that's why I look familiar."

"Even though I have a B.S. degree in Business, I work as a maid for a major resort." Lisette paused. "Hold up. If you don't know me, why the sudden interest in my life?"

"I'm sorry. I didn't mean any harm, Lisette."

"Wait, how do you know my name?"

Realizing her mistake, Keita stammered, "You must have told me."

Robert called out, "Kieta! We need you back here." She took the opportunity to get away from Lisette, "I'm coming."

Lisette dropped her head. "Kieta, wait! I'm sorry for snapping at you. I just have a lot on my mind and I guess I forgot I told you my name." Lisette became uncharacteristically emotional and with the weight of her brother's life in limbo, she began to feel sorry for herself. She thought about how her life would have turned out if she had gotten the job in New York that was perfect for her. But once they did a background check and found out she lied about her past, it was a wrap. She didn't mean to mislead them, but the thought of losing yet another opportunity because of a past she couldn't even remember, was nauseating.

Now that Lisette was all alone with her thoughts, she reached for the only thing she knew, prayer. "Lord, you know I did wrong in the past. Please make a way for me to get that job as a project manager. I've made some bad decisions, but please help me to forgive myself, so I can put the past behind me. Let your name get the glory. In Jesus name."

Emotionally spent, Lisette cried herself to sleep. The dream came hard and fast. It was so real. She heard tires screeching and could smell smoke. She felt the impact of the car hitting something and an eerie sound of crunching metal. Then there was blackness. She couldn't see anything, but she could hear everything. "Oh, my God, what are we gonna do? I think he's dead."

Lisette began to thrash in her sleep. In the dream she heard her brother's voice. "We don't have a choice. This could be my third strike and you could lose your scholarship." The female voice was crying hysterically. No matter how hard she tried, Lisette couldn't open her eyes and see what was going on around her.

Noticing Lisette's thrashing, Kieta hurried over and shook her. "Wake up!" Lisette opened her eyes and stared in shock. She gasped for air like a woman drowning. Keita's voice sounded just like the one in her dream. Could that be how she knew her?

Captain Baker spoke over the intercom and interrupted the exchange between the two women. "Attention passengers. The delay is over. We will begin to follow the schedule as planned. We will be taking off shortly. Please take your seats and buckle up. Thank you."

Lisette's phone rang. It was Nikki again. "Where are you?"

"I'm heading that way now. The delay is over, and we should be taking off shortly."

"Matt needs to talk to you."

"Okay, put him on the phone."

"Lizzy," Matt whispered. "Lizzy, I am so sorry."

She could tell he was crying. "Matt it's okay. Just tell me what happened."

"Lizzy, I'm sorry. Please forgive me."

"Forgive you for what?"

"The night of the accident . . ." The phone went silent.

"Hello? Hello!" Lisette screamed. "Oh Lord, no, my phone is dead!"

Robert rushed over to calm Lisette down before she incited panic. "Are you okay?"

"No, I was talking to my brother. He was trying to tell me something about the night that changed my life, and now my phone is dead. Do you have a phone I can use?"

"Sure." Robert reached into his pocket, grabbed his phone, and handed it to Lisette. Lisette quickly dialed Nikki back. "Nikki, my phone went dead. Let me speak to Matt. He was talking about the acc . . ."

Nikki interrupted her sobbing. "Lisette! Matt is gone! He's gone!" Lisette grabbed her chest because she thought she was going to have a heart attack. The tears flooded her face like a waterfall. She couldn't manage another word and simply hung up.

Robert and Kieta were standing in the rear of the plane watching the tragedy unfold. Robert decided to go to her. He sat beside her in the empty seat and grabbed her hand, "What's wrong, miss?"

"I'm sorry," Lisette said. "I just found out that my brother died. He was trying to tell me something that happened ten years ago. I don't get why he kept saying sorry, and now I'll never know! Then, earlier, I had a dream about it. It's never been clear to me, and all I can remember about that night was me, Matt, and his girlfriend were all at a party together, drinking, smoking, and dancing. I was driving and a young teenager was killed. I was convicted of manslaughter and served two years in jail."

Concerned and shocked, Robert reached for Lisette and gave her a hug. "I am so sorry, Lisette."

Captain Baker announced over the intercom. "Attention passengers. Will everyone please take your seats, and buckle up. We are getting ready to descend. Thank you all for staying calm and for your cooperation during our emergency landing. I hope you have enjoyed your flight."

As Robert continued to comfort Lisette, he looked back at Keita, who was wiping tears from her face. He had known Keita a long time and empathy was not her strong suit. Something about this didn't add up.

When the plane got to the gate, Lisette gathered her carry-on and headed into the airport terminal to wait for the rest of her bags. Kieta followed Lisette out and was watching her from a distance. When the last passenger left the plane, Robert headed out to find Kieta. He approached her and said, "Kieta let me talk to you. What do you know about the situation with Lisette? Something is not right. You told me you used to live in Daytona Beach, and that it's been ten years since you saw her. If you know something about this, you need to make it right. Right now, too many people are hurting. Lives have been destroyed from secrets and her brother died trying to confess. I'm telling you, you need to make it right."

Kieta bit her lip and she struggled with a truth that was a decade old. They saw Lisette grab her bags and making her way towards the terminal exit. Kieta ran to catch her. "Lisette, we need to talk."

Lisette was not in the mood. She just wanted to go home. She snapped, "What do you want!"

"The reason I knew your name is not because you told me, but because I know you. I'm Charlotte Donaldson." Lisette stared at her incredulously. "I know I lied earlier. I had to. You don't understand." The pieces were beginning to come into place for Lisette. She dropped her bags and got in Kieta's face.

Through clenched teeth she asked, "What do you know about that night?"

Kieta took a step back, "Listen, we had to stick together that night. You didn't kill anybody. I was scared. I had my whole life ahead of me. I had just received my scholarship to college, and we didn't want to go to jail."

"Spit it out, Keita. This is not a game."

Tears began to roll down Keita's cheeks. "On the night of the accident, Matt put you in the driver's seat."

"What!" Lisette screamed.

"I know. I'm so sorry. At the time, it seemed like that was the best. You were still a minor and Matt and I both had something to lose. I realize now how selfish we were, and how you're still paying for it after all this time."

Lisette slapped Keita so hard she fell on the floor. Lisette was in unimaginable pain. Being betrayed by someone was always a crushing blow, but being betrayed by your own family was paralyzing. She began to take deep breaths and she noticed that she was causing a scene. Robert rushed over to help Keita to her feet. Lisette looked into Keita's dazed eyes and said, "You will be hearing from my lawyer! You will clear my name. For years, I beat myself up over the fact that I made a decision that cost an innocent person their life. You cannot imagine what that's like. I spent two years in a juvenile facility because of you and my own flesh and blood."

Keita only responded in tears. Lisette demanded, "Who was driving?" No response. "I said who was driving?"

Keita whispered, "Matt." It was a kick in the gut to Lisette. Keita could see how much it hurt her but there was nothing to be done about it now. Matt was gone.

Lisette picked up her bags and through tear-filled eyes she said, "This was a divine intervention. I cannot be grateful for it and harbor bitterness in my heart. I'm choosing to forgive you and my brother because you will reap what you have sown. He can get you back better than I ever could. Good luck with the rest of your life. You're gonna need it!" Lisette strutted out of the airport, finally free.

Robert looked at Keita and said, "Well, that was intense. What happened between you two?"

"Nothing to concern yourself with. I'm a survivor and it doesn't matter what she does with the information I've given her. Once again, self preservation is paramount."

Robert wished he had heard their entire conversation, but he had the feeling Keita was not one to be messed with. As they headed back to the plane, Keita thought back to that night. Matthew was so in love with her. He would do anything, including betraying his little sister. She was the driver that night, but she convinced him that of the three of them, Lisette was the only one who could stand to take the legal hit. She wasn't worried about her lie though. The only one who could contradict her story would soon be six feet under. Once again, she had gotten away with murder.

Robert shook his head at Keita's cockiness. He wondered how long it would be until life dealt her, her own wicked twist of fate.

2. A Wicked Twist of Fate, Angela Y. Hodge,
   angelayhodge@gmail.com

3.

There Are No Mountains in the Bronx

John McPhaul

Lisette Donavan stood at the Long Island Railroad Station. In an evening rain and hiss of passing traffic, she awaited a bus to an apartment we shared in the Bronx. Against the chill of November, she stood tall and lean, pushed the hair from her face, and folded her arms across her chest. At twenty-eight, traces of tough times were yet to detract. Now, far from the manicured lawns and mansions on Long Island that employed her as a house cleaner, she appeared callous, as grim as the darkened skies. The truth is, for Lisette, happiness was a face not recognized and peace, gazed only from the bottom of a gin bottle.

"Why did I come to New York . . . to continue to take this crap from Nevel Teddington, and allow him to touch me?" she grumbled. An old lament, one she knew too well. When the cross-town transit arrived, she merged into a line of anxious commuters, boarded a crowded bus.

"North Carolina," she once said. "The death of my daughter; these are the memories that still imprison me. With malicious intent," they said, and then sentenced me to ten years. God only knew, and it was God who sent me to prison."

I first met Lisette in a Harlem bar, a November night, three months after Armstrong's first steps on the moon. Alone she sat.

"Give me a light," she demanded. "Are you from North Carolina? Clooney's here is a hangout for a small group of North Carolinians. Expatriates, someone called us. Imagine that, we're expatriates." She gave a muttered attempt at a laugh.

With her drink in hand, it didn't seem to matter who, or if, anyone was listening.

"Give me a light." She repeated herself, pulled a fresh cigarette from her purse, zipped it shut, and penned it again between her body and the bar.

"Didn't I see you here last week?" I asked. As certain as I was, I didn't want to appear emphatic.

"I was."

"You wore a blue blouse, long-sleeved, with black slacks. My name is Simon. I'm a cabbie. And no, I'm not from North Carolina."

"Lissy Donavan," she introduced herself. "Seen your share of characters, I suppose?"

"I like what I saw that evening. Later, I dropped you off at the Greely Hotel. You don't remember that, do you?"

"About the cab ride or was there something else? You seem like a nice guy. That all you drinking, a beer?"

"Maybe, might work another shift, but one is enough. You staying at Greely's again?"

"Yeah," she answered. "I work on Long Island, come in on the weekends. It's what I do at the moment, but before long, I'll climb that proverbial mountain, plant my flag, and stake my claim to success."

"Simon, you from Manhattan?"

"No, I was born in the Bronx."

"Family?" she continued. Her eyes searched my hand for a wedding band, then focused again on my face.

"I'm not married, if that's what you mean." I chugged the last of my beer and cast a long, sultry glance before saying, "You own that color, blue, should always wear it. Any trace of blue will align anything you wear." Her long, shapely legs had not escaped my gaze and her waist-length leather jacket lay open to a protruding sweater-clad bosom.

"Listen, I have a place nearby. Why don't you join me for another drink, relax—when you're ready, I'll drive you home?"

She gave me the once-over, ground out her cigarette, then licked her lips.

"Sure," she said. "Let's go." I laid some bills on the bar, and we weaved our way toward the door.

In my first floor flat, I quickly undid some untidiness, and welcomed her in. I had only a bottle of Clan McGregor Scotch and a few beers to drink. Lissy poured scotch for herself and settled into my arms. I made my moves and she allowed me—kissed her and she kissed me back. The taste of gin and scotch fueled the roar inside me, but she was calm and composed. Suddenly, she spoke of her past, her childhood, Indigo, North Carolina, and a man named Teddington.

"My hometown," she said. "Stood by a huge hunting preserve, owned forever by the Teddingtons. Of four lodges, one was a stone's throw from my home. I was fifteen when Mr. Teddington lured me there, suggested I be the caretaker. A tall, skinny man he was, with close eyes and large teeth; gave me a bottle of beer, asked if I had a boyfriend."

"You know what boyfriends are for, don't you, Lissy?" Mr. Teddington had asked.

"His eyes mauled my body, the quiver of his lips wished to say what I knew he was thinking."

"Boyfriends take care of their girlfriends. Have another beer, relax," he continued.

"He tried making me comfortable, but I knew what he wanted. Soon the alcohol or someone took over my body, perhaps an older woman wanted to show a child how to be grown. Then he handed me another beer."

"Do you and your boyfriend have sex?" he asked.

"Just like that, he asked, like it was his business. Nevel, I said, but it was the beer and the older woman speaking; how old are you?"

"I'm thirty-seven. And how old are you?" he asked.

"Sixteen, I lied, as if he cared. Mister, what I do with my boyfriend is none of your business. So easy it was; a few beers, calling him by his first name, and I was in charge. I was grown, and he let me be as grown as I wanted to be. Nevel grabbed me and kissed me, fondled every place his hands and arms could reach. Then we did it. I let him in, the devil—I let him in and to this day,

I'm not sure who, Nevel, or the older woman inside me, changed forever my life. Inebriated, I cussed like an enraged whore. I handled Nevel, gave only what I wanted and how I wanted. As much as he had his way, he smirked at my ability to minimize his wishes."

A faraway look in Lissy's eyes matched the plea imbedded in her confession, interesting, but ill-timed. I tried changing the subject, appealed to whatever compelled her to come along. She welcomed my search among her soft contours that rose and fell in her breathing. We stood as she hung her arms around my neck, and I guided her to my bedroom where again she confessed, "I'm not good at this."

I heard only the scream in my loins as I continued to search among her wonderful things and found my way. Lissy's eyes never closed, fixed as they were on the ceiling, she allowed me, but shared nothing.

"I'm sorry, Simon," she later said. "I tried to warn you. I've been through so much."

"No, Lissy," I whispered. "I'm the heel." Only then had I begun to understand her pain. I held her for the real love apparently she never received, kissed her as if it were the breath of life. For one night, I was her lover, then, forever the sharer of her burden.

"I'm a big girl, Simon. You don't know anything about me," she said softly. She stood and went into the bathroom, then the kitchen before returning with a drink for her, a beer for me, and climbed back into bed.

"You don't spend much time here, do you?"

"No, I'm . . . gone. Lissy, I have an extra room. It won't cost you anything. Take it, no strings. Be sure to remember me when you climb that mountain, stake your claim to fame."

"You can't be serious. I mean nothing to you."

"Stay tonight. We'll get your things from the hotel, take the bus back . . . no strings."

She sat up in the bed, one leg folded under her, the other outstretched. Her blouse, open, exposed her wonderful bosom while she contemplated my offer. There was no shyness in her nudity. She did not flaunt it but seemed oblivious to the effects of its arousal.

"Don't get mushy on me, Simon. Don't feel sorry for me. Maybe I took advantage of you. I'll consider your offer, but you think about it, too." We got dressed, headed for the hotel.

A week later, I came home to find Lissy sitting on the stoop, holding a glass of scotch.

"Hey, guy! How you doing? Before you get upset, I jimmied your door lock. Don't worry, everything's alright."

"You jimmied my lock?" I asked, surprised and happy to see her. "You jimmied a police lock! Lady, we're in the wrong profession."

"Six years inside," she said. "You kinda pick-up skills."

"Simon, I can't say how much this means to me." She finished her cigarette, exhaled, and thumped it to the curb; then, we both entered the apartment.

"How long you been here?" I asked, opening a bottle of beer.

"Four hours," she answered. "Come here, Simon, see what I did to the room."

With rearrangements, Lissy added a woman's touch. "What do you think?" She asked, pleased in her efforts.

I looked, nodded approvingly, then said, "It looks good, Lissy. I like what you are right now, happy; look at you, you're smiling."

She approached me, laid gently her palms on my chest, but gave no clue if what she wanted was a warm, supportive embrace or a kiss of fire.

That Lissy was a beautiful woman was a given, her ebony skin, huge eyes, and long legs. I struggled in my objectivity for she was careless in her nudity and often inflamed my abstinence, but privy to her past and struggles with Nevel Teddington's possessiveness spelled clearly the love and friendship she needed.

"Now you're going to treat me like a big brother." She said, "Worry about me. Maybe you should hear the rest of my story."

"At sixteen, I was pregnant," she shared. "Nevel was furious, and I cussed and handled him to appease my guilt. Then he mentioned the one woman in town whose craft everyone knew."

"You take care of this or find your way to Sade's." He screamed.

"Abandoned, I was a child again, left to explain this, or go see Sade. I waited until I was showing, until mama caught me puking one morning. Still I would not tell who. Before my 17th birthday, my baby was born—a girl and as white as clabbered milk."

"My older sister, Becky, cornered me."

"Lissy, who is this baby's daddy?" Becky pleaded.

"Silently, I sat with the Hunting Lodge in sight. Summertime, its insects, the smell of pinesap from the lumber mill nearby, painted the air.

"Leave me alone, Becky," I said. Few expected me to measure up to her or Neal, my younger brother. Patient was Becky, supportive but fascinated by details that eluded her these past months.

"Girl, you gotta tell somebody something. Mom and Dad's hearts are broken, and you are going to need help raising this white baby. I wanna help you, Lissy. You can't carry this alone. "

"I ignored her, gazed at the lodge next door. When I saw Nevel, I walked over."

"I thought I told you to get rid of that child! What are you thinking?" Nevel snapped.

I looked at him, something was different. Rarely had he resembled the snarl of southern white men, but that day, his was the look of evil.

"You get rid of it, or I'll see to it," he said, huffing toward the door. "I ambled again across a well-worn path of sandspurs, entered the house, and unconsciously listened for the squeak of the screen door closing behind me. In need of repair, the door would drag across the top step, then, a squeak of the hinge signaled its closing."

"In my silence, tongues wagged about town. Sparingly did I talk to God, but thanked him for my Mom and Becky. "

"Becky aroused me from a familiar stupor."

"You better get yourself together, girl. That's your baby in there!" The secrets angered Becky more than my insensitivity.

"We're going for groceries and dry-cleaning. You want to come?" she asked me. "You need to get out of the house."

"I got laundry and the baby's asleep," I replied. "Go ahead." In the late afternoon sun, I heard sounds of quail hunters and hounds at a distance, heard the baby crying inside. I hurried into the house, gave it a gentle, cooling bath to stop the crying. I tried to feed it and like Mama, I laid it against my shoulder, rocked it gently, but nothing would stop it from crying. Then I cried. In a rage, I began breaking, throwing things. I looked at it . . . then I lost it; thrown into madness, I decided to choke it—choke my hand close around its tiny neck. I must have fainted, fallen to the floor for the screaming trailed-off. I opened my eyes to hear the signature slide of the screen door and squeak of the hinge, heavy feet descending the steps. Said to myself, *they are back, Mommy and Becky's got the baby, stopped it from crying.* I dragged myself into a chair, wondered where everybody was? Haggard, tired, and depressed, I could not remember a thing."

"Lissy! Something is wrong with the baby! This baby ain't breathing!" Mom cried.

Screaming, now, she repeated herself. "Somebody, call the ambulance. Oh, Jesus! Oh Jesus, look at this!"

"We can't wait!" Becky yelled. "We're going to the clinic!" My feet would not move, my eyes still glued to the floor.

"Why are you sitting there! What's wrong with you, girl?" Both Mom and Becky screamed yet again.

Then they were gone again, to the clinic, to the hospital, I don't know where. They returned and again shook me from my stupor.

"What did you do, Lissy . . . what did you do?" Becky cried.

"Jesus . . . help me, please! Help my child!" My Mom winced as Dad prayed in the bedroom, and Neal sat with his face in his palms; on TV, a sportscaster reviewed a baseball game.

"Lissy, what did you do? Lissy, my child, did you . . . I can't believe this," Momma cried.

I shook my head, hoisted my open palms, but could only say, "I ... I ... I ... it just . . . happened." The next day, two officers came to the house.

"Ola Donavan? We need to see Ola Donavan," one of them said. My mother joined them, closed the screen door, its drag, and its squeak. Mumbling sounds, unintelligible waffled through the screens. Then she screamed."

"Oh . . . no . . . Jesus! Please, God, not my baby!" I heard my mother cry.

"We have to take her with us. There will be an arraignment in the morning," one said.

"Charged with involuntary manslaughter, tried, then sentenced to ten years in prison, I served but six. Nevel later financed my college wishes then invited me to New York. Said he would help me get on my feet. I took the job last June as house cleaner."

"Nevel's attacks began last June," she continued. "In the very same house as his paraplegic wife, he forced himself on me and I pummeled him, left and right, until I learned he was a sick and perverted man. The pain I inflicted was the source of his jollies. In his nakedness, black n' blue, limping and bleeding, he took me at will, reveled in the stimulant of pain, force, and his ability to dominate me.

"A bank account," she continued, "Was the carrot he dangled before me. Only his signature or death released the funds. There's enough for me to scale that mountain, Simon, plant my flag and stake my claim," she said. "I fought him, never gave in, and became a zombie. I seduced you the first night we met, Simon. I wanted it with someone of my choosing, on my terms—see if I could ever be whole again. You and I know I have a ways to go yet."

December, seven months after arriving in Long Island, Lissy's tragic string of peaks and valleys ended.

"On the first floor, he came after me," she began anew. "He pinned me to a wall and without a struggle, I told him he could never really have me, and he went ballistic.

"I can kill you! I can kill you the way I killed that mongrel child of yours! Now, does that put any fight in you?"

I stood frozen, shocked. I always thought someone else was in the house that day, heard them leave, and heard the slide of the screen door and squeak of the hinge.

"I should have killed you, too!" Nevel said.

"I sensed he was capable, so I bolted upstairs towards his wife's suite of rooms. At the top of the stairs sat a tiny, antique table used to horde cash in large denominations. In a rage, he raced after me. Seeing as I was removing the money, he yanked the table from my grasp. When I let go, he went reeling towards the bottom of the stairs. Mr. Teddington! I cried, then, gave out a blood-curdling scream. Mrs. Teddington's nurse emerged from an upstairs room to see the mangle of man and table below.

"Mr. Teddington has fallen down the stairs!" she cried.

I never saw Lissy again. She phoned to say, "I'm going back to Indigo, start over again—climb my mountain, Simon, stake my claim. "

"It's good you're leaving," I said. "What you're needing, you won't find in the Bronx."

3. There Are No Mountains, John McPhaul,
   xuannam66@embarqmail.com

4.

Empty Pockets

Laurina Osborne

It's hot as hell under this bed. Today of all days, I'm caught up because my past just won't let me go. I saw him, and my greed got the best of me. It always does. And when it does, it overrides every bit of common sense. Of course, my twisted brother had to agree with me.

I grin, remembering the smell of money as he walked past me and my cleaning cart, pretending he's nobody. I watched from under my lids, the way he handled the bellboy, and the confidence he exuded. The man's got money and I, Lisette Donavan, know just how to relieve him of it.

Trust me. I've tried to be a better person—to get beyond my pickpocket past. I even went to college and walked out the front door with a bachelor's degree in Business Administration. But have you seen what a regular paycheck looks like? Pursuing the American dream takes hard work and sweat. And if I'm sweating, I better have something to show for it. And with my brother Robbie's help, and my sister's genius, I'm doing alright.

But who wants to just do alright? I'm a maid in this hotel for a reason. Cleaning up after nasty people is a dirty job. Relieving them of something they may never miss makes up for it.

He leaves the room, and I use my key. Before I could think about what to take, he's back. Under the bed is my only option. He enters and drops across the bed. I wait and wait, then text Robbie to tell him about my predicament.

I wait fifteen, twenty minutes . . . an hour. If this man doesn't leave, I'm gonna scream.

My phone lights up. It's a text from Robbie. He says the door to the adjoining room is open and to leave through there. Do not use my key. I get ready to text back and he moves on the bed. It's time.

"Hello," he says, and I wait.

"Okay, I will be there in . . . five minutes. What if the phone is in use?"

He waits, and I wait.

"Okay."

His feet hit the floor. He's wearing black gold toe socks. His feet are big, looks like a size seventeen. I knew a guy once with big feet. He was fat though. I really liked him.

What the hell? His briefcase almost hit me in the face. I ease over before it could touch me, and I can't believe it's this easy. My hand hovers over it, but I pull back as my eyes catch his hands tying his shoelaces. Those are expensive shoes. I hope this briefcase pays off. He stands and faces the bed, then turns, and walks five steps to the door. He stops, his shoes point back at me, and I hold my breath.

Don't change your mind. Leave it here. It's safe with me.

He slams the door, and I breathe in and out quickly. I count to ten and then pull my body from under the bed with the case attached to my hip. I unlock the adjoining door. The room is empty and not yet . . . cleaned. It was cleaned, but Robbie must have messed up the bed just in case. I grab all the towels to cover the case and let myself out. I drop the case into a big, grey garbage bin conveniently located outside the door and keep walking. The room service cart is a step away, and I climb under the table fixing the white tablecloth in place. There are no cameras on the floor, but just in case someone passes, they would not see me.

Robbie's singing as he pushes the cart and pulls the garbage bin. I hope what's in the case is worth singing about. He wheels us onto the elevator. I stay put until the door opens again and I feel the rush of cold air. The wheels of the cart protest against my weight and the concrete floor.

"Get out and get back to work. I'll let you know. Michele put you on kitchen duty for disappearing."

I give him a look. Michele is the hotel manager, his girlfriend, and my best friend. Somebody must have complained that they had to clean my rooms in the hour I disappeared. I drag the wig off my head and shove it into my locker, then pull on a hairnet and brace myself to hear Mrs. Larchmont call me a lazy good-for-nothing the same way she does every time I'm relegated to kitchen duty. Why should I pretend I want to do what she asks when what I really want to do is stuff a potato down her throat and watch her gag on it?

"Why the hell doesn't she just fire you?" Mrs. Larchmont yells in my face before my shoes hit the kitchen floor good. She jams the handle of the knife into my hand and point. "Don't let me hear a word outta you or you'll be washing dishes the rest of the day."

"Yes, Ma'am," I say with a grin on my face. I'm anticipating what's in the briefcase, and she cannot keep me down, not today.

At the end of the day, I catch the bus home without hearing from Robbie. We don't usually talk about business at work. As soon as I find a seat, I feel my phone vibrate. It's Michele. I get a bad feeling. She knows my schedule, and if she's calling me now, it has something to do with the briefcase. Robbie should have taken care of it. It's his decision what happens after I turn it over. He may decide to take everything and return the case empty or just take what may not be easily missed and return it under the bed.

Fifteen minutes later, my phone vibrates again, and it's a 911 text from Michele. I get off the bus four blocks from home and call her.

"What?" I scream as soon as she picks up.

"Do not scream at me, Lisette Donavan. Did you take a good look at the face of the man you robbed?"

"Of course not. They all look the same to me," I say laughing. "Rich and in need of unloading."

"It's Ian Lawrence."

"Who?" I say and swallow hard. "It's not. He's . . . he's . . . fat," I say choking back tears.

"Not anymore. Lissy, you have to come back."

I lean against the fence of the vacant lot that's littered with garbage. I close my eyes tightly and stoop to the ground clutching the phone. I feel myself becoming hysterical.

"Shellie, I am not going back to prison and especially not for him. Robbie has the case. Give it back or keep it. I don't care. I'm not coming back," I say calmly, and shut the phone.

I should've known. Those big feet can only belong to one man. I see them again the way I saw them from under the bed, long and slender, size seventeen. I loved his feet more than I loved his fat chubby body. My butt touches the sidewalk and tears leak down my face. I see the bus coming, pull myself to my feet, and quickly dry my eyes. I don't care. I'm not going back. I feel my phone again and quickly turn it off as I find a seat on the bus.

I look out the window as the bus crawls under the tracks of the El. I can't believe I take this damn slow bus home every day. I get off at the next stop and start running. My feet hurt, but I run. The thought of jail usually gives me a rush, but not today. I run in front of a car, hear the screeching of the tires and his horn, and I run faster.

I stop at the gate to catch my breath and fumble in my bag for my keys.

"Lisette, is something wrong?"

"What?"

"Is something wrong? You're huffing like you just ran a mile," my nosy landlady, Mrs. Pine, says.

"Nothing's wrong. I can't . . . can't find my keys," I say panting.

"I have mine, I'll let you in," she says, and I follow her down the sloping driveway and around the side of the two-story house. She opens my door.

"Thank you, Mrs. Pine," I say and slam the door shut as I slide around the kitchen table, knocking over the chair and jerking to a stop in the bathroom.

I scramble out of my coat, toss it behind me, click on the light, and puke again and again into the toilet. My breathing is fast as I hold the bowl and stare into the grey frothy stink. I well up, and my tears mix with the vomit. I'm shaking. My whole body covered in cold sweat. I flush and hold back my head, willing my body to stop shaking. I'm still breathing hard as I crumble to the cold, tiled floor.

My father's face swims in front of mine. He's old and wrinkled in his minister's collar. 'God never gives you more than you can handle.'

"God always gives me more than I can handle, and this time I'm outta here."

I scramble to my feet, step on my coat, and walk past the windowless box that's my living room. I switch on the light in the adjoining guest room, and my eyes dart around the room for my suitcase. The bed is buried under clothes and cardboard boxes. Stuff covers the floor. It's my overflow room; at least, that's what I tell everyone, including Mrs. Pine when she does her annual inspection. Actually, my cash is stashed in a broken down suitcase under this mess. I push clothes off the bed until I see it.

I hesitate. Someone's knocking on the door. I listen, and it stops. I pull at the case again, and the knocking starts again. I tiptoe to the kitchen and carefully pick up the chair. My hands are still weak and shaky and I shake them as I continue on to the door. I put my eye to the peephole.

It's Robbie.

I'm not going back.

He pounds on the door again. I carefully step back and hurry to the bathroom. I wash out my mouth and pick up my coat. He's still pounding, and if I don't let him in, he'll go to Mrs. Pine. His name is on the lease. So I let him in.

"I'm not going back."

"Lissy, you have to. Someone kidnapped his daughter and the ransom money was in the briefcase."

I pull out the chair at the kitchen table and sit down. I rest my head on the chair and close my eyes. My head hurts. I open my eyes and Robbie's charcoal eyes are staring back at me.

"This was your idea. Find a way to give it back. I'm not going back to jail and I don't want to see him."

"Lissy, I have an idea. The old woman is dead, and maybe all this happened for a reason. You can use this to see Margaret."

My heart gallops fast. I jump out of the chair.

"I don't want to see her. She's his daughter, and didn't you say she was kidnapped?"

"That's what he told Michele. Michele promised him the hotel will make good on the money, even though we're not obligated to. When he checked in, he was offered the use of the safe for his valuables, and he refused. He's frantic and he can't go to the police. The kidnappers warned him not to."

"Good. Give him back the money as if the hotel replaced it."

"I think you should pretend as if you took it on purpose, so you can see Margaret. Make a deal with him."

"I don't want to see her," I say quickly and scramble back into the chair. "Rob, why would anyone kidnap her? I know they're rich, but why her?"

"He thinks it's kids. They only asked for fifty thousand dollars, but he's following the rules just in case. He had a tracker in the case, which I dropped back under the bed with the empty case."

"Rob, it's your turn to take one for the team. I'm not getting involved."

"Lissy, you are involved."

"I don't want to see her and I'm not confessing to stealing his money."

Someone bangs on the door and my heart speeds up again. Rob sees the fright on my face.

"It's probably Michele." He stands up, looks through the peephole, and lets her in.

She glares at me and I glare right back. I'm sick of the two of them ganging up against me. I went to prison for them, and I'm not doing it again.

"No!" I scream. "It's someone else's turn. I'm not . . . I'm just not . . ." I say as I lower my head onto the glass table.

"You have to. If something happened to Margaret, you'll never forgive yourself."

"I will. I had nothing to do with her kidnapping."

"You swore that if you ever had the chance to see her you would say all the things you never got to say. Lissy, baby . . ." she says hugging me. "Please, do this for you. You love her and she's in trouble."

I nod and squeeze Michele tight. She's the only one I ever told how I felt. Michele and my journal somewhere in that old attic know everything.

"Okay," I hear my voice say.

They wait while I shower and change. If not for those metal bars on the windows, I'd be long gone.

Thirty minutes later, I'm sitting in the car next to Robbie, looking as if my bachelor's degree is finally paying off. I exchanged my white shirt for a blue blouse. This navy blue suit always does wonders for my olive skin. I grab Robbie's hand just in case it's the last time. He's my brother. He knows me.

"What are you going to say?" he asks, squeezing my hand. I don't answer.

He hands me a bag; it's the money. For fifty thousand dollars, I don't mind getting hurt jumping out of a moving car. I still see the old woman's face when she took Margaret out of my arms. I was fifteen, and she kept me in that attic for six months until I gave birth. She had my father's permission. His family had money, and I swore I would take it all one day. I couldn't take theirs so I took everyone else's.

"Lissy, in the conference room," Robbie says. I nod and step out of the car in front of the hotel as if I'm a guest.

I'm a big girl. I owe him nothing. If anything, he owes me. I will hand over the money and leave. I don't give a shit what he thinks. If he had killed his grandmother like I asked, we could have raised our daughter together; instead he let them force him into some boarding school. He gets a daughter and the mansion, and I get a jail cell and empty pockets.

I push the hate out of my body through my mouth and lick my lips. I reach for the door with sweaty hands. I turn the knob and push it. There he is; he's thinner, but his face is unchanged by time. I prefer him fat. His eyeballs bulge with surprise and recognition.

"I knew you would come," a voice says from behind the door. I slam the door shut and turn toward the voice. I swallow; tears come to my eyes. She's his daughter.

Thirteen years ago, I swore to that old woman I would never claim her. I won't. She looks like him.

"Lissy, this is Margaret." I turn away from her and face my father. He's old. His minister's collar is missing.

"You set me up? How could you?" I ask as tears run down my face.

"Margaret set you up. She found me and persuaded me to find her mother. Ian refused to help and when I brought her here to New York City, to this hotel, to meet you, we both witnessed you pick a man's pocket. Margaret thought it was the coolest thing ever and I . . . well you know me . . . I had to kneel at your mother's grave and ask her to intervene."

My legs have had enough standing for one day, so I slowly walk to the table and pull out a chair. I sit down and shove the bag of money in Ian's direction without looking his way.

"You are my mother, right?" Margaret asks from behind me. I cross my fingers and shake my head, no. I close my eyes tight. "You gave birth to me."

I nod and open my eyes.

She grins.

I close my eyes. *Thank You, God. I will never steal again, I promise. Thank you.*

"Can you teach me how to pick someone's pocket?" she asks, her thirteen-year old voice an echo of my younger self.

"Over my dead body!" Ian's voice bellows out, filling the room. Another echo. Those were his last words when the old woman gave him that ultimatum. Give me up or else.

I smile big.

4.   Empty Pockets, Laurina Osborne, laurinao@yahoo.com

5.

You Can Never Leave

Melinda Michelle

She awoke with a scream in her throat strangling her. Her body was covered with her fear and perspiration. She thought her heart was going to beat out of her chest. Lissy began taking deep breaths. This was becoming a normal occurrence for her the closer it got to Halloween.

She turned on her bedside lamp. The images that flashed through her mind tormented her. She needed to purge herself of the grave memories that haunted her subconscious. She reached into her nightstand drawer and pulled out her leather bound journal. She opened it to the next blank page as her fingers played over the ripped edges of the previous pages that were torn out. Her mind was plagued, her soul burdened, and her body weary. The images from the nightmare came in flashes.

Twelve bodies cloaked and hooded in black. No faces shown. The plot in their hearts unknown to me. Black burning candles. Chanting and worship of the dark lord. I worshipped . . . until. Frightened look on her face. Her bare body tied to the altar. The ancient athame glinting in the moonlight. The inhuman wails she made as her body was sacrificed. The blood. Her last breath. The shame. I'm a coward. Not an animal sacrifice.

She shuddered at the memory as she tore out the page and got out of bed, her night gown clinging like a second skin. She avoided the mirror as she headed out the bedroom door. What was the point? She no longer looked like herself anymore. She was someone else. Her hair color, eye color and even her name were all less than a year old. She had been born full grown at twenty-eight-years old, ten months ago.

She navigated through the sparse one bedroom apartment to the shoe box sized kitchen. She had been there six months, and she was not impressed with the infamous city of New York, but that could be due to the demons she'd brought along with her.

She turned on the stove and waited for the eye to get hot. She placed the corner of the torn journal page on top of the now glowing red eye of the stove as she had done with all of the previous pages. She watched as the flame crept quickly to the top, not even flinching when the heat neared her fingers. She was used to it; her fingers were now immune to the pain.

The ashes fell to the stove as she reached to turn on the light. When she turned back, an image of a snarling vicious barking dog head appeared before her. She screamed and fell back into the fridge as it disappeared. Then she heard the voices in her head chanting, "You can never leave."

Lisette Donavan, as she was now known, managed to get one additional hour of sleep after her ordeal the night before. She was average height with a small curvy frame; her previously vibrant light gray eyes were now a sad brown. Her once long auburn hair was now a short choppy black against her caramel skin that was now spotty and shadowed due to stress and fatigue. She was used to living her life on little sleep, especially since it was only three days until Halloween. The feeling was bone deep that they would find her and she would be the sacrifice to the dark master this year as payback for the betrayal of her coven. Barely able to contain the tremble of her hands, she headed out to clean up after others, thanks to her new career as a maid for a temp agency.

The job, a daily reminder that this was her fault, a path she chose. It didn't matter that she had a bachelor's degree because college didn't teach you common sense. She had to get herself together because she was moments away from having a nervous breakdown.

According to her psyche evaluation, she suffered from "middle-child syndrome." It acted as the catalyst to seek attention. At first, she just got involved into the gothic look to get noticed. But then she attracted the wrong crowd. One thing led to another and before she knew it, she was a member of a coven. If that didn't get some of her parents' attention from her star athlete brother and her goody two shoes sister, nothing would.

They say hindsight is 20/20, and she thought there had never been truer words. Tears welled up in her eyes as she thought about her family. Lisette had no clue if her family even knew she was dead or alive or even if they cared. It didn't even matter if they cared, she would gladly go back to being the miserable middle child if it meant she could escape the mess she had gotten herself in.

She had decided to contact her case officer, Agent Holloway, of the FBI, to let him know her life was truly in danger. She hated him. He did his job as far as protecting her but not a thing more. Coffee in hand, she stood at the curb waving down a cab as she searched for her cell phone in her purse. A cab finally stopped, and she slid in and gave him the address to the temp agency as she dialed.

He barked, "Yeah, make it quick."

Lisette rolled her eyes, "And good morning to you, too."

He let out a grunt.

"Listen, I'm really worried about the holiday coming up, and I think we should change our routine for at least the next week." She was mindful of what she spoke in front of the cabbie even though he probably barely spoke English. She continued. "I've been getting messages from my old friends, and I think they want to meet with me face-to-face."

The cabbie made eye contact with her in his rearview and made her squirm. It also made her paranoid because she didn't trust anybody, including the agent on the phone, but she needed him.

"What do you mean by sending you messages?"

"I can't exactly get into those details right now. Let's just say they got their point across."

He sighed. She knew he never put much stock into the coven having actual power, but just as she had once believed God was real, she knew the devil was, too. In her mind, one could not exist without the other. She, however, deeply regretted switching teams.

"Look, Agent Holloway, this is very real and even if you don't agree, it is your job to protect me, so I'm telling you we need a new plan."

The cabbie was taking too much interest in her conversation and while she didn't think he was a demon sent to kill her, she had a weapon for flesh, too. She slid her hand in her coat pocket to where her MPA Protector .380 sat patiently waiting for its debut.

She told him to keep his eyes on the road, and he seemed to get the hint. Agent Holloway said, "We actually wanted you in a different location this week and have already cleared it with your agency. You will have a new assignment today, and we will send in two UC's to cover you for the next three days. If you spot them, you are not to acknowledge them unless you feel your life is in danger, is that clear?"

She said sarcastically, "Sir, yes, sir," and hung up. It felt a little better to know that undercover agents would be watching her back.

The cab driver pulled up to the curb of the agency as she paid him without a tip for being nosy. She took in a deep breath of the crisp fall air and was filled with regret. Regret of all the times she hadn't told her family that she loved them. The pain of being away from them was making her believe a minute long contact was worth the risk. Witness protection was not the glamour that TV would have you believe. She couldn't wait to testify and be done.

Lisette stood at the curb and just like the past two days, the same cabbie pulled to the curb. She was running late, so she couldn't really wait around for another, as there never seemed to be one anyway. She glanced to her left and saw the two UC's in their unmarked vehicle. She had made them on day one, but was more dependent on her .380. She hopped in and in her perpetual state of loneliness; the familiar face of the cabbie gave her a small comfort. She couldn't explain it. He kept quiet, as always, though she did ask him his name yesterday. She said, "Hey, Jamaal."

He nodded and pulled into traffic, comfortable silence enveloping them both.

Working for the Longfellow's residence for the past two days went without incident. He was a lawyer and she was a spoiled exotic beauty with nothing to do except boss her staff around and spend her husband's money, as far as Lisette could tell. Today was Halloween and although she was jittery, she was well rested because the night before she had slept more soundly and peacefully than she had in months, and she could only attribute that to the first prayer she had uttered to God in years. She thought her name had long been crossed out of his book, but she was so desperate it led her to fall on her face and ask for forgiveness and help.

In a better mood, she was looking forward to her new assignment in the house, the master bedroom. She entered the elaborate room, and her skin prickled. Fear gripped her like an iron fist around her throat. She felt another presence in the room, even though she was alone. She slowly turned to look around the room as a flash of silver caught her eye. She couldn't remember to breathe as she approached the sterling picture frame. The blue-eyed beauty staring back at her was the young woman who had been sacrificed one year ago to the day.

She wanted to scream. She wanted to run. Most of all, she wanted out of this nightmare. She felt dizzy. What was going on? Did Agent Holloway know whose house this was? She sat down on the side of the bed and put her head between her legs and began to take slow breaths. She heard the door creak but couldn't bring herself to look.

Mrs. Longfellow said, "What is it? Are you alright, dear?"

She stood and said, "I'm sorry, ma'am. I felt lightheaded."

The woman walked to her.

Lisette said, "May I ask about your daughter? I just saw her picture, but I haven't seen her around the house."

The lady reached for the picture and held it close as a tear trickled down her face. "This is my heart. She's been missing for a little over a year now. She went out with some friends and never came home. I keep her picture near me as I continue to pray, it seems in vain, for her safe return."

Lisette made an audible gulp. "Why do you say in vain?"

She sighed, "Because a mother knows. I know my child is dead, but until I have a body, I don't have to accept it."

The guilt, fear, pain, and confusion struck Lisette like a sledge hammer to the chest and she was about to confirm this woman's worst nightmare when the doorbell chimed. Mrs. Longfellow quickly wiped her tears and headed down the stairs. Lisette followed. When she opened the door, Lisette recognized the two undercover agents, one male, one female standing at the door.

Mrs. Longfellow said, "Yes, can I help you?" The woman pulled out a weapon; the muffled shot hit her point blank in the chest and she went down. Lisette screamed and turned to run as they walked. The man took aim. she felt a pain in her back and everything went black.

When she came to, she was surrounded by darkness, her hands and feet were bound, her mouth taped, but she knew she was in a moving car. The realization of being locked in a trunk immediately produced a cold sweat, and she realized she had been praying subconsciously. She could hear the tires' steady pace against the asphalt. Come on, Lisette, think. She felt around trying to get into her pocket to see if they took her phone. She couldn't reach it or her .380 that was taped to her back; she knew she was in serious trouble. It was Holloway's men that attacked her. Oh God, did they kill that poor woman? She felt nauseous as it struck her that her soul was being required tonight. The vehicle began to slow down minutes later.

She felt the bile rise up in her throat as she reached around to find anything. There had to be some kind of weapon in the trunk, something! There was nothing. The trunk opened and she saw the evil faces of her captors. As she stared with horror in their eyes, she could literally see murder in them. She had to fight for her right to exist.

The woman reached down and cut the ropes that bound her ankles. Lisette was about to kick when the man shook his head and pointed her .380 at her head. *So much for it still being taped to my back.* They pulled her out of the trunk and flanked her as they began to walk. She looked around and all she could see was a cabin in the distance; everything else was woods and more woods. She prayed as the tears rolled down her cheeks. She knew they were going to sacrifice her that night but the darkness had already settled in. Time wasn't on her side.

They made it to the cabin, dragging her unwillingly along. He opened the door and threw her on the couch. The woman slammed the door. The room was only lit by candles and a kerosene lamp. Suddenly, there was a rushing wind that blew the door open, causing all the candles to go out. The kerosene lamp fell and shattered as she heard the two agents hit the ground. She saw a shadow in the doorway. She was petrified until she felt a reassuring hand pulling her out of the darkness and into the moonlight. She looked up to see Jamaal as he was cutting the ropes from her wrists. As she removed the tape, she asked, "Oh my God, what are you doing here?"

"Shhh, we have to hurry. They're just unconscious."

Once again, she felt a sense of peace being with him, and she took his hand as they began to run towards the road.

As they made it to the clearing, Agent Holloway stood pointing a gun at her. Her heart stopped along with her breath and her feet. Hate filled his eyes as he said, "Our secrets will die with you tonight on an altar screaming."

Even in her fear, she had one single question for him. "Why did you send me to that poor girl's house?"

His smile was evil. "Longfellow represented the whore I married in our divorce, and he took everything from me. Now he's the one with nothing!"

Her heart broke for that family, but the only person she could help now was herself. She knew he didn't want to shoot her, but sacrifice her, so she had to find a way to play that to her advantage.

Bright lights and a gun came out of nowhere. Someone yelled, "Drop your weapon!"

Jamaal pushed her down and covered her with majestic wings that sprang out invisible to the human eye. Men in tactical gear came down out of trees as they were surrounded. Holloway refused to comply. The shot that took him out was deafening.

Even with all the chaos going on around her, she felt completely safe and at peace beneath Jamaal's protection. She had no idea how long he had covered her but when she opened her eyes, she saw her family rushing towards her. Tears streamed down as she ran to their embrace.

Lisette said, "I'm sorry, I'm so sorry."

Her mother said, "It's okay. None of that matters now, you're safe."

She stepped out of their embrace and said, "I have to find Jamaal. He saved me." She went up to one of the officers and asked, "Where did Jamaal go?"

The officer stared at her blankly, "Miss, I'm not sure who you're talking about, there was only you and the nut with the gun."

She stood there dumbfounded. "No, he's my cab driver. He saved my life."

The officer patted her on the shoulder. "Miss, you're in shock. You should get checked out."

She walked back to her mom confused. "How did you guys get here?"

"We were contacted by the FBI, and they told us everything and brought us here. They mysteriously received all the evidence to convict and try all 11 members, including one of their own."

Her dad said, "Agent Holloway was a high priest."

She stared at the body in disbelief. It had been a setup all along. Her grandmother always said, "The devil didn't care anything about you," and boy was she right!

The officer walked to Lisette and said, "Miss, there is no cab driver by that name that works for Yellow Cab, nor did we find a cab. You must be mistaken."

She fell to her knees and wept because she knew God had sent an angel to protect her. She knew then that no matter what she could never leave *Him* again.

5. You Can Never Leave, Melinda Michelle,
    gwendolynevans21@yahoo.com

6.

Last Date with Elijah

Thomas R. Wilson

"Pretty Black girl like you. You look too smart to be a hotel maid."

Lisette glimpsed over at the man on the moderately crowded subway platform: Caucasian, dirty, with the cobbled together wardrobe of someone used to living on the streets. He wore an Army surplus winter jacket that might have been his own, with a grey hooded sweatshirt underneath. His teeth were blackened, and mostly missing, and his hair was matted. He could have been thirty or sixty.

"I know a fish out of water when I see one," he said. "You might want to close your coat. It's cold, even down here. God bless you!" He moved away to panhandle the other commuters, who tried to ignored him.

Lisette began to button her dark, knee length wool coat that she wore over her Waldorf Astoria uniform.

A train was coming. Lisette stood in the center of the platform and was amazed at the way some of the people stood at the very edge. As the large, silvery snake rolled into the station, she reached into her small clutch purse, and pulled out ten one-hundred dollar bills. She walked over to the homeless man.

"Excuse me, Sir!" she called. She tapped him on the shoulder. "Here. This is for you. You're right. I am a fish out of water. Bye-bye!"

The door of the train opened. Lisette joined the lemmings inside. Of course there were no seats, so Lisette stood. As the doors closed, she saw the vagrant look at the bills. He locked eyes with hers, half in shock and half in awe. She smiled at him and waved good-bye as the train pulled away from the station.

Lisette already knew the city, having spent her summers and some winter breaks there with her Aunt Mary. Aunt Mary was a Holy Roller and she would drag the young Lisette all over for "the Lord's Work." But the Heavenly Itinerary consisted of trips to Broadway shows, museums, Coney Island, zoos, and ice skating in Central Park. Oh, yes, and occasionally to church revivals as well. Lisette never revealed her Aunt's secular identity, not even to family. But she had once told Elijah.

Elijah.

She and Elijah were childhood friends, having grown up in and around the insular world of the Talented Tenth of Jacksonville, Florida, in a world of African Methodist Episcopal (A.M.E.) churches, National Association for the Advancement of Colored People (N.A.A.C.P.) youth rallies and small tastes of forbidden fruit when the grown-ups weren't around. Their romance had finally begun in their senior year of college and continued while they settled into their careers, Lisette into elementary education, and Elijah into law enforcement. But when her mother died, she postponed their marriage plans to try to straighten out her younger brother, Lance.

Lance was supposed to have outshined Lisette, but after high school he ended up living with one of his so-called friends. He claimed that they were going "into business." She never asked why the two young men moved into a single-wide trailer down a dirt road, a few miles outside of Jacksonville proper. Once every two weeks she would deliver groceries to the hovel, which smelled of musty young men, unwashed dishes, and a lack of ambition.

She remembered the last Saturday she had seen her brother alive. As usual, she knocked on the door at noon, her hands full of plastic grocery bags. The blinds opened slightly, followed by rustling and the rapid unlatching of the door, which swung open. Her brother stood inside, wide eyed, and looking past her.

"Lisette, you got to go, NOW!"

"What's wrong?"

"Nothing! Is that food? Don't need it! Now leave! No, wait!" He stepped out of view, then came back with a brown paper grocery bag, half-full but rolled down, and sealed with silvery duct tape. "Don't worry, it's not dope! Now get the hell out of here!"

"Lance, what's . . ."

Unblinking, he reached in his pocket and pulled out a pistol. Slowly, he lifted it toward her forehead and almost whispered.

"Lisette, I love you, but you gotta go. Thanks for trying to help!" Instantly, he lowered his arm, snatched her in a hug, and kissed her on the cheek. Without saying another word, he pushed her away and slammed the door in her face. There was nothing else to do, but to leave. She stepped over to the hand-me-down blue Suburban that their father had given her and climbed inside. The engine was still running; without looking back through her tears, she drove away.

"It's me!" Lisette said, locking the front door behind her.

She shared a brownstone apartment near Columbia University. As usual, their living room was strewn with half-done art projects: masks, paintings, and books. Christie was a slender Korean graduate art student who wore skinny black jeans, Andy Warhol-inspired t-shirts, flip flops, and an ugly black and red wool cap that had long, wool ear flaps. She never seemed to be cold nor neat; after two years, Lisette had long since given up trying to rehabilitate her sloppy friend.

"Did anybody call?" Lisette asked.

"Just Elijah. He said you never answer your cell phone," Christie said. She entered the room, carrying a bowl of something that looked like noodles and melted cheese. "For a guy who's getting dumped, he sure is persistent!"

"Tell me about it," Lisette said. "By the way, did you open the envelope I left for you?"

"No."

"It's been two weeks. Open it!"

The 21 Lives of Lisette Donavan   55

"Lisette, I'm not worried. You always pay your share of the rent."

"Open it now!"

Christie stepped over to the bulky, older, unwatched television, which sat atop a short, light brown wood cabinet. With one hand, she lifted the corner of the set, and snatched a plain, orange manila envelope from underneath.

"Satisfied?" Christie said as she opened the envelope. "You're not like my last roommate, who never paid—" Christie pulled out a neat stack of bills, all hundreds. "What's this?"

"That's my share of the rent until the lease runs out."

"Wow! Where do you get this kind of money?"

"My mother's life insurance policy."

"So what if I decide to run off to Atlantic City or Vegas?"

"I'll catch you," Lisette said with a smile. "Remember, my ex-fiancé is a cop!"

Lisette walked down the hall to her room and unlocked her door. Inside was a neat cubicle containing only her bed, a dresser with a large mirror, an old wooden desk, and an overflowing box of used books that were starting to multiply. There was a window, but all she saw were bars and a brick wall. She had always hated the lack of a view and looked instead at her reflection; she found someone who was too young to be tired, too neat to be frumpy, and too attractive to be ugly. Yet all three she was: A very tired looking, modern day Nefertiti in an ill-fitting domestic's uniform.

On the desk was a large portrait of her family. Her father looked a little like Bill Cosby, only skinnier; her mother was an older version of Lisette. Lisette and Lance could have been twins, though they were separated by one year. They had taken the portrait just before Lisette had gone away to Florida A & M University. But she forced herself to look away. This was before her mother took ill. This was before Lisette's father abandoned her mother on her deathbed. This was before she learned that not even the love of a good man could heal open wounds.

Elijah.

Elijah's picture was also on the desk, but Lisette refused to look at it. Lisette closed her eyes like her mother had done to stave off the sickness brought on by chemotherapy and loneliness. But for Lisette, there were no prayers to be uttered; only the deep exhalation of inevitability.

She unlocked the drawer under her desk with an old, brass key on her key ring. Inside was the paper bag her brother had given her, still rolled down but with the tape stripped away. There was a stack of white, stamped envelopes in the front, along with a stack of money orders from different banks and stores. Casually she thumbed through the orders and went down her mental checklist: A student loan payment, a gift for her Aunt Mary, one for Christie with Happy Birthday! written across the top. There were others, but she stopped at one for Elijah. Above the printed, five-hundred dollar amount were the words she had written weeks earlier: I love you. I'm so sorry. Good-bye.

Hastily, she slipped the checks in their respective envelopes, bundled them with a rubber band and placed the completed stack back in the drawer, which she closed, and locked. She was amazed at how smoothly the mechanism latched on the old desk. Elijah had taught her about WD-40.

She wanted to throw-up. Instead she grabbed a fresh towel and bath cloth from the top drawer of her dresser and reached for the pink robe that was hanging on the back of the door.

She replicated her daily subway route back to her job at the Waldorf, ascending near Columbus Circle, across the street. It was now night and the icy air pinched at her face. On street level, the traffic hadn't lightened one bit as the vehicles—mostly cabs and an occasional horse and buggy carrying tourists—passed by. The trench-coated workers on the sidewalk had evolved into socialites, newlyweds, and cart vendors. Lisette felt alone, isolated.

A deep voice spoke from behind her.

"Ice skating in the middle of winter! This is supposed to be romantic?"

He was tall, dark brown, and appeared rather underdressed in black jeans, a leather jacket, and a scarf. He wore a black and white wool cap with a white bob on top that made him look silly.

But his hands were sheathed in a pair of expensive, black leather gloves, which she recognized as the pair she had given him.

"Elijah!" Lisette said. She hugged and kissed him and wanted to go further. But then her nausea returned.

They crossed the street and walked along the edge of the park. Elijah seemed to glory in the fact that he knew someone who worked at the Waldorf, and he prattled on about all the cultural references he knew, from the Muppets' to some crocodile movie to Eddie Murphy. Lisette was thoroughly uninterested, but she held his hand and pulled him closer when she felt the chill of the slight breeze.

"Anyway, they seem to think that us single deputies don't have lives. We've been working double shifts, due to budget cuts. But I put my foot down. I told Sheriff that either I got this week off or I quit."

"You're too much of an ass-kisser to quit!" she said.

He paused and truly seemed insulted. But instead of retaliating, he only smirked, and shook his head. Lisette saw the scratch on his forehead, where she had once thrown a rock at him, when they were little. Most people would never have noticed it.

They walked further and turned down into the park. The walkways were brightly lit by globe lights atop the poles, which softly illuminated the snow-dusted, dormant grass. Up in the distance, two police officers walked leisurely on their beat. There were other couples approaching and passing, and Lisette felt jealous of them all.

After a short distance, she began to hear the not-so melodious sound of contemporary pop music: Wollman Rink. For years, Lisette thought it was, "The Woman Rink." Spectators watched from outside the perimeter while the winter-clad skaters sliced, sailed, skimmed, and occasionally fell across the ice.

Lisette was about to reach for her purse, but Elijah stopped her.

"I got this!" he said. He pulled out a hundred dollar bill and paid for them both.

"You know you don't have to do this!"

"Yes, I do. Since you're dumping me, I want to make you feel as guilty as possible! Besides, I gotta do something with this money you've been sending me—which, for the record, I'm still begging you to stop!"

"I told you. It's from my mother's life insurance."

"Sure."

The entire floor inside was covered with thick rubber squares that fit together with the precision of jigsaw puzzles. While Elijah opened their locker, Lisette unzipped her boot-like carrying case. Reverently, she stared at her Aunt's white hand-me-down skates, which were lovingly preserved and perfect. Meanwhile, Elijah plopped down with his rented pair, an ugly brown set of blades that looked worse than bowling shoes.

"Time to get some fungus!" he said.

"They spray them," Lisette said.

"I hope so. By the way, I spoke with Mr. Rogers at the Funeral Home. He said it was a pleasant change to not have to hound people about their bills."

"That's nice!"

"Oh, and your parents' old house is fine. I keep the grass cut, and the hedges trimmed, and your father still pays me. He wants to rent it out. But I've been thinking about getting him to sell it to me."

"He can do whatever he wants!"

Now laced up, Elijah stood atop his blades, straight and tall. It had never occurred to Lisette to ask whether he could skate. But he led her almost too fast out onto the outer deck (also rubberized) and toward the gap in the rails. Gently he invited her out. She followed and they glided around the circle, away from the other skaters who were passing, slowing, falling, and circling. Up above was the glow of floodlights bathing the now hazy night. It was probably going to snow.

"I meant it when I said I couldn't marry you," Lisette said, softly.

"And I meant it when I said okay, as long as you told me why. But you never did. Tell me, is it because you don't like me?"

"Actually, sometimes I don't," Lisette said.

"And as usual, you haven't told me why. What? Are you scared I'm going to blackmail you?"

Lisette dragged her toe brake and stopped.

"Look, Elijah! I can't stand it when you talk in circles!"

He stepped back a bit, as if to allow her to see his full frame. His face was now sober, almost cold. He reached inside his jacket with his right hand, as if reaching for his gun. But he pulled instead a set of papers, folded.

"This is a copy of the final police report. We knew there was a meth operation in the area, but I didn't know Lance and his friend were involved. Apparently, they pissed off the wrong guys. Rough dudes, too. We caught them on a routine traffic stop. Strangely enough, we never found any money, either on them or at the trailer. But we did find two bags of groceries on the ground. I never told anyone what you told me. For the record, everyone thinks that you went crazy and ran away."

"I swear. I didn't know there was money in that bag. I still have most of it. You can arrest me, if you'd like."

"I can't arrest anybody. I quit the force a month ago."

Lisette lost her footing and fell to one knee. Her nausea disappeared but was replaced by resignation. She sat on the ice. Her coat was thick and she felt no cold, but an icy chill spread down her spine. She felt fear toward the one person left who she knew still loved her. But when she looked at him, she only saw the kindly smile of her best friend, her comforter.

"So what are you going to do?" she asked.

Balancing on his blades, he carefully helped her up. By now more people had joined them on the ice, as the music swelled into a corny, old fashioned waltz.

"Now that I am unemployed, almost broke, and an accessory to a cover up," he said resolutely, "I am going to figure out how to convince my money-laundering, ex-fiancée to marry me. So tell me. What are YOU going to do?"

"I'm going to do THIS!" she said.

For the first time in a while, Lisette felt like smiling. She let go of his hand and skated backward toward the center, slowly at first, then executed a move that her Aunt had taught her. She threw herself into a lazy single axle with a small jump and turn. Elijah stood where she had left him. Gaining speed, she swung by, and tried to kiss him but missed. No matter; she blew it to him anyway. Once again she returned to the center and began to spin in a slow layback.

There were better skaters nearby, mostly pre-teen girls, and she knew they were snickering at her bad form and lack of technique. But she didn't care. As she completed her third turn, she looked upward into the haze, into the night, feeling free, and finally accepting the love that had already been given to her by family, now gone, by Elijah, now here, and by the forgiving Judge up above, on High...

6. Last Date with Elijah, Thomas R. Wilson, Tallahassee Writer@yahoo.com

7.

Gettin' My Happy

Xavier D. Woods

Christian Maxwell Blaine was the debonair assistant hotel manager of our New York midtown establishment and my new boss, a too-good-to-be-true blue blood of a brotha who was out- of-my-league on every rung of the social ladder. That meant a romance deprived sistah like me didn't stand a chance with the likes of a Blaine. Didn't matter. I deserved a Christian in my life.

"Lissy, will you get your mind off that man and back on vacuuming this lobby?" JoyLee politely chastised, as she caught me starring at Christian for the umpteenth time that month.

I smiled at my wonderful and nonjudgmental sister. The grin was my thanks and appreciation for her getting me the job. JoyLee was in year eight as head of housekeeping, which meant I had a job as long as I didn't continue to screw up my life.

"I'll stop looking when he quits looking!" I playfully added, and pivoted around and leaned my five-four, slender frame into the handle of the purring vacuum cleaner; providing my future boo-to-be a full view of what one-hundred squats and lunges every other day could do for a sistah's behind on a size six frame. JoyLee shook her head in loving disapproval.

"Is he going to the Christmas luncheon Saturday?" I managed to sing over the hum of the vacuum. I knew the answer before she let out another breath. Christian was presenting the annual Hotel Employee of the Year award at the party; and JoyLee had won it for the first time in her tenure. I was co-presenting at his request. He didn't have to ask twice. Shoot, he didn't have to ask me anything more than once!

My sister yielded a quiet laugh. "He always does, sweetie. He always does." But a sudden look of concern started to darken her lovely features.

"Lissy, baby." She made her way over as I quieted the vacuum. "Understand that I only want what's best for you and Nathan."

JoyLee had been mother and father to my twenty-eight-year old twin brother, Nate, and I, since our parents passed some ten years ago. We owed her more love than we had to give.

"But this infatuation you have for Mr. Blaine," JoyLee said, easing to quiet again. "I just think your attention should be on getting yourself together and starting over." Now whispering, "Once your record is cleared."

I turned to minimize the sting of her maternal words. I started to tell her how sorry I was for the fiftieth time. That I knew she was right, but then I found Christian's beautiful face smiling in my direction from across the grand lobby. My heart soared; so did my hope.

"Big sis, you know the difference between you and me is that you see Mr. Blaine as your boss." My perfect teeth, purchased at my former real job, fortified my confidence. "I see him as just Christian. He already knows about my recent troubles, right?" Now waiting for her to confirm what she told me the day I was hired.

"Mr. Blaine knows everything. I've told you that," she quickly added.

"And knowing what he knows about my past, he still shows all of this interest in me!" I proudly proclaimed.

JoyLee shook her head in motherly concern. "That's because you're beautiful, and unfortunately, have more butt than brains."

She glanced at my slightly snug uniform and rolled those caring eyes. She dropped her head near my ear.

"And Lissy, don't forget, in this impossible fairy tale of yours, you're in no position to claim wrong doing, because he holds all the cards in whatever game you wish to play. That puts you at a man's mercy, baby. And no woman wants to be in that position. Remember?"

Her words yanked my recent sordid past into our present. I swallowed, and stated with less confidence this time. "I can handle him."

JoyLee exhaled and gently pulled my silky, shoulder length hair to the side.

"Momma's hair. You and Nate got hers, and I got daddy's wooly mess!" she teased, then kissed me on the cheek. Her eyes went sad again.

I felt the need to ease her melancholy. "I thought fraternizing among employees was frowned upon Miss Queen of Maids?" I jokingly added in weak consolation to her worried expression.

"Somehow," my big sister added, "I don't think *that* part of hotel policy concerns you!" She nodded with a wistful smile and started to stroll away. "Careful Lissy," was offered in sisterly love or as a warning. It didn't matter which.

JoyLee was the kind of sibling you were blessed to have in your life. Nate was the kind of relative you would gladly trade for a six-pack of diet cokes and a goat. I loved my brother as much as I did JoyLee. But worthless should have been his middle name.

It matched the middle name of every man I had dated the last five years. And I was tired of putting in time with the worthless. Tired of feeling like I was serving pittance for relationship sins I didn't commit. Fed up with always being the reason *we* didn't work. At least that's what the losers in my life tried to feed me. Now my only friends were ex-boyfriends, who were more reflections of past ills than anything else. But I was rectifying the situation.

Christian was mine, whether he wanted to be or not. He wouldn't have a say in the matter. We were going to be made for each other, or we were going to hurt for an eternity. Live in love or live in misery. There would be no in between. I had no more time for doubt in my life. Desperation was my motivation, just like my motivation for school.

Got my bachelor's degree by dating enough fools with the money to afford me. I loved for cheap; tossed aside my dignity for a formal education. The users kept me in cash to get started in a research medical career. Rushed through the courses to graduate before I needed a chiropractor to fix all the things I allowed them to do to my body; or a psychologist for what I let them do to my mind. Only the medical technician degree, with my name adorning the expensive sheath of higher education paper, was as useless now as an eight-track player. I quickly grew tired of working with bacteria and germs in the too cramped and dingy research lab in lower Manhattan. Really didn't need a degree for that mindless, low paying job.

"You have to crawl before you walk in that research role Lissy." That's what JoyLee had preached to me when I voiced frustration with the lab job seven months ago.

"Not if you marry well!" I had replied, when I smirked at my big sister's career advice.

I had dated enough parasites to keep the Center for Disease Control in business for years, so I knew one when I kissed one. Rashaun Duncan was my personal parasite. Taught me stealing was just another economic pillar of capitalism. He didn't have to work too hard to convince me. Stealing and conning was a hell of a lot more dignified than sleeping with the parasites I had allowed in my life. The fake promise of love was all the collateral Rashaun needed for the down payment on my heart.

His con was foolproof. As a PR gesture, my company started donating old electronic balances to equipment-starved local high school science departments. It was my responsibility to identify and select the schools for the used electronics. A few dollars to an underpaid administrator or two at a school, and they would sign off on receipt of a used electronic balance that was worth a few tax write-off dollars to the firm. On the street, the balances were worth a thousand dollars apiece.

"Can't have the brains of the outfit on lockdown, baby!"

That's what my lover and sorry parasite of a partner yelled over my work phone before scurrying out of town just ahead of the law. Forty minutes later, I heard my name oozing from the mouth of a badge toting Irishman.

"Lisette Donavan?" The police officer's question had been more of an order than a proper query. "You're under arrest for . . ."

Never heard the rest as my co-workers froze in stunned surprise. I only felt the coolness of the metal jewelry adorning my then shivering wrists.

Rashaun had managed to get involved with one of our dozen or so bribed school administrators. She wanted more *of him.* And after two months of juggling the both of us, he dropped her. Vengefully, she dropped his name to Crime Stoppers.

Because I was a first time offender and since the firm didn't want the pub of being associated with putting drug equipment on the streets of Harlem, they made sure the DA's office treated the thefts as a misdemeanor. The DA's office agreed to one charge of petty theft of one set of drug scales for my cooperation, if I provided the names of the school administrators we had bribed. My selective memory recalled one person. I gave them *the her* my parasite lover had been involved with.

The prosecution agreed to clear my record if I could keep my nose clean for six months. The best way to do that was with a Q-tip or a good man. And I wanted to stick Christian Blaine anywhere he could fit on me.

So here I was again, staring at Christian in the lobby of the hotel, praying for a blessing I knew I didn't deserve, willing to sell any remnants of my soul for the chance to make him mine. The question was how much soul did I have left to barter?

"I'll drop the plaque off around 6:00 P.M., Mr. Blaine." I cooed into the cell and wished I were whispering directly into Christian's ear. "Sorry, it took so long to get it done, but this is the only time I can see you to review it and make sure everything is okay before the awards presentation tomorrow."

I couldn't get to the hotel before six anyway. Needed time after work to inhale enough to squeeze into a dress I wouldn't be able to fit in after the holidays.

"That's fine, Lissy," he replied, with less interest than a gay man at a female stripper's convention. "I'm in the hotel bar with one of my boys," he casually added. "He's taking me out to meet the fellas for a short celebration."

"Congratulations! Celebrating your promotion?"

Earlier that Friday morning, Christian received word from the corporate offices that he'd been promoted to Regional Manager. The formal announcement was to occur at tomorrow's Christmas luncheon, after we presented the Employee of the Year Award to JoyLee.

"But, Lissy, you're off duty, right?"

My throat constricted from the rush of anxiety.

"You really don't have to make a special trip to bring the plaque on a Friday night. We'll have time to rehearse our speech tomorrow."

No way Christian would ever be mine if I couldn't see him tonight. "It's not a problem. I have a date around 8:00 P.M., and we're meeting near the hotel anyway. So just have a drink on me, and I'll see you in a few." I held my breath and prayed for the response I needed to hear.

"Alright, Lissy. I'll have that drink, and we'll have a quick practice when you get here."

The immaculate hotel lobby was overflowing with the after-five Friday evening work crowd. I sighed upon spying Christian, and slowly made my way through the masses toward him and his friend.

"How long is this going to take?" Christian's guest inquired after gulping a large portion of his oversized margarita.

"Not long, about an hour. You go ahead and tell the fellas. I'll see you in a bit. Need to brush up on the speech Lissy drafted for the Christmas luncheon."

"Who the heck is Lissy?"

I sauntered in from behind a group of leering junior executive types, whose lustful intent provided enough camouflage to keep me just out of Christian's line of sight. He wouldn't have noticed me anyway. He'd never seen me in dressed-to-seduce mode.

The backless v-neck, black, satin dress hid nothing; except my deepest decadent thoughts. I had cautiously loitered within earshot, waiting for this opportunity.

"Hello, Christian!" My salutation was as planned as a premeditated murder. The sway of my hips was all the introduction the friend required.

"Dang!" his boy mumbled under his alcohol-tainted breath. He should have sworn. The evening dress I wore would make a minister compromise his faith.

Christian's slight head bow was chivalrous. But his smile was a sneer from a thugged out gangsta. If he had licked his lips, I would have stripped on the spot.

"Hello, Lissy," he whispered. "Nice dress. Do you have the plaque?"He asked without taking his eyes from the goose bumps adorning my lean and exposed shoulders. This was still New York in December. And to give the dress its full effect, I had draped a shawl about my arms and waist. It explained why my fist was closed and tightly clasping the shawl edges, as well as my future.

"I put it in your office," I softly added. One of the benefits of housekeeping meant my master keycard gave me access to most rooms in the hotel. What I needed was the key to his desire.

Christian nodded, the gleam in his eye signifying an interest he could never publicly express.

"May I?" I took his hardly touched apple martini and turned my back to him and his gawking buddy. I surveyed the wall of people mingling in the lobby. The hotel's Friday night happy hour was a known spot for midtowners.

"Shall I make a toast, Christian?" I said, addressing the throng of hotel guests I hoped to never have to vacuum for again in life.

The continued informal use of his first name made him chuckle again; the laughter making the nape of my neck tingle. His mood confirmed a growing sense of comfort between us.

My eyes were on the lobby and the sea of mingling bodies. But my mind was nine months ahead, knowing my future had just begun.

"A toast to who and what?" his non-factor friend spoke to the smoothness of my bare and backless dress.

I turned and faced the newly appointed Regional Manager. "To Christian on his promotion. To this Friday evening. To the present season, and mostly, to the three seasons yet to come!" I raised the glass and handed it back. Christian's expression was one of confusion as he reclaimed his drink. His eyes locked on mine; my desperate intent as clear as a wordless expression could convey.

"Then to the seasons," he added as he took a gulp of the martini.

"And to us?" I quietly and desperately added.

Christian Blaine chuckled lightly, but his indifference was real. He held his head eschew so as not to cast any disrespect directly in my face.

"I'm sorry, Lissy, and I don't mean to come across as rude but . . ." His eyes trailed to the cleavage pouring out the top of my much too revealing dress. My breast held his attention. Tonight, they were doubling as a pair of aces in a poker game of sexual tension. I was gambling, and maybe losing. He took a shallow breath of disinterest, and I knew the words to follow would do more harm than good. "But I don't think we should go there. We do work together, after all."

Wish I were deaf. Then I wouldn't have heard the soft dejection from the flawless pitch of his wonderful voice.

"Oh, seeing someone?" I asked, so I wouldn't have to drag my tainted dignity out of the lobby before complete embarrassment consumed me. He smiled and no other words followed. I nodded, knowing what was behind his closed lips was an unspoken, 'Ain't no *way* we going there!'

I lowered my head, personal shame dragging my self-esteem floorward. "Then I'll see you in your office. We can rehearse the speech and look over the plaque."

Christian's voice softened, "Lissy, I didn't mean to . . ."

I smiled up into his apology; my head slowly turning in silent resignation. As I turned and moved toward his office, I heard his noisy partner add to my departure, "She ain't yo' type no way."

The friend's mock snicker caught the back of my ears. My eyes stayed ahead, my mind calculating the economic certainty of my present. I knew I didn't meet Christian Maxwell Blaine's country club standards, but the price of the two ecstasy pills I slipped into his drink were still in my budget range. So was desire for him, and a better kind of life and existence.

As JoyLee had reminded me, fraternizing among the staff was not permitted. The newly appointed Regional Manager of our hotel chain would do anything to keep his good name and new position intact. My shaking hand reached for the door latch to his office. But what was next for Christian and me?

Marriage? Hopefully. The emergence of a weak smile found the corners of my lips.

A baby? My first after tonight—if I knew my body clock. And I did.

A bribe from Blaine? At the very least. And that was an art I had mastered. A recently jailed school administrator would attest to that.

7. Gettin' My Happy, Xavier D. Woods, southwood3716-2@comcast.net

8.

Wrong Turns

Irma Clark

"Lisette Sharee Donavan."

I held my head high as I walked across the stage to receive my degree. It felt so good to hear my name among the college graduates receiving degrees that Saturday morning. I knew I looked like a professional woman with my shoulder length black hair freshly permed and trimmed. I'd often been told how well my jet black hair complemented my pecan-colored skin.

Finally, I told myself. *I've earned my Bachelors degree in Social Work.* I was so proud of myself, especially since I graduated *summa cum laude*. My mother always said that I could do anything I put my mind to. She was right. Yeah, it took me awhile to get it, but at the age of 28, I'm still proud of myself. I got sidetracked with life, but as the Bible says, the race is not given to the swift but to he who holds out to the end.

I waved to my family in the audience: my mother, father, brother, sister, cousins, Lisa and Jennifer, and of course, Aunt Rose, my main inspiration. Aunt Rose had no children of her own, so all of her nieces and nephews were her children, and she was determined to help us make something of ourselves.

After graduation, my family wanted to have a celebration dinner for me. I had other plans. I wanted to spend the day with friends. Since tomorrow was Sunday, I convinced my family that we could have our celebration on Sunday after church. I was surprised at how easy it was for them to agree with me. Now, I regret putting my family aside. Had I not given them a rain check,

I would not have made such a mess of my life. After learning a hard lesson, I have my priorities in order.

After graduation, I headed to Imperial Restaurant to celebrate graduation with my friends, Carla and Rhonda. We thought it fitting to celebrate at Imperial because it was one of the finest restaurants in New York City. We had only been there a few times because it was a bit pricey. Since we had just earned our degrees, we felt we deserved to splurge a little.

"Let's get the party started!" Rhonda, the bubbly one, yelled as soon as we were seated at our table. It seemed half the graduates must have been at the restaurant with their families and friends because the place was some kind of crowded and noisy.

"First round of drinks are on me," announced Carla. "After that, everyone is on her own."

"That works for me," Rhonda and I stated in unison. The three of us had spent a lot of time together because we were the oldest students in most of our classes. Rhonda was flying home to Chicago tomorrow and Carla was driving to Tampa, Florida, where a job was waiting for her as a social worker at the hospital where her brother was the Director of Human Services. My plans were to remain in New York City with my family.

"Remember, you can always come to Tampa if nothing works out for you or if you get tired of the snow and want to enjoy the Sunshine State," Carla informed me. "I'm sure my brother and I can help you find something."

What about I find your brother or he finds me. Kill two birds with one stone . . . get a fine job and a fine man at the same time, I told myself. Carla's brother was two years my senior and just as single as I was. The love of his life walked out on him three weeks before their scheduled wedding date—because she found someone she thought was more exciting. Well, she left a good man for someone else, hopefully me.

"Earth calling Lissy," Rhonda called out as she waved her hand across my face. "There you go, spacing out on us again. Penny for your thoughts. Never mind. As usual, you're not going to tell us."

I didn't think that every thought that ran through my head was meant to be shared.

After filling our bellies with delicious food and spirits, we headed our separate ways.

Rhonda and Carla were riding together. I drove myself because I was going to the other side of town to my parents' house to spend the rest of the weekend with them. I was planning on going to church with them in the morning and then spend the day with the family to celebrate my graduation. As I headed to my car, I felt a little tipsy, but I was sure I was quite capable of driving the short distance to my parents' house. Rhonda and Carla warned me to drive carefully.

"Don't worry. I got this," I told them. That's one of the last things I remember about that day.

Three days later, I woke up in intensive care with my father standing over me. "Well, well, Lissy, you are the first person I know to get your bachelors degree, total two cars and a movie theater, back over a policeman's foot, and take the police on a high speed chase all in the same day."

"Be easy on her, Robert," my mother told him. "She needs our love and support."

I'm convinced that man never liked me. 'My little black sheep,' he sometimes called me. Don't hate me because my brother, Reginald, went to college on a football scholarship and was drafted by the Green Bay Packers and last year, my sister, Samantha, graduated high school two years early and went to college on an academic scholarship. Of course, my father rubbed it in my face two years ago when my sister received her Ph.D. in English and is now teaching English at the University of New York. It doesn't help that I am the oldest and my younger siblings have gone so far and I'm just getting my degree. I think my father was counting on me getting a basketball scholarship. I think it was an insult to him when I quit the basketball team at our high school where he was head coach of the boys' basketball team. He was determined that since I was tall like him, two inches shy of six feet, I should be a basketball star. I played basketball my first two years of high school, but I lost interest halfway through my junior year.

"I guess you'll think twice about getting behind the wheel of a vehicle after drinking," my Dad told me.

My heart was pounding. What was he talking about? Then it began to come back to me. I remember the road getting a little blurry and then seeing police lights behind me. I was hoping I was just in their way and they were trying to get to someone else, so I moved out of the way. When I changed lanes twice and the police changed lanes, too, I knew they were after me. It didn't help that my tag had expired three weeks before. Honest, I was planning on renewing it the following week, but I guess that wasn't soon enough.

A week later, I was released from the hospital and ordered to report to the police station immediately. My parents drove me to the police station without a second thought. I was arrested and released on my own recognizance. My driver's license was suspended, and I was instructed to expect a court date in the near future for a judge to decide my fate.

Three months later, I found myself standing before Judge Thomas Madison. The look in his eyes told me that he did not care for me at all.

"Lisette Sharee Donavan, I find you guilty of aggravated assault on a law enforcement officer, driving under the influence, destruction of property (two cars and a movie theater as my father so rudely informed me when I woke up from a coma), and eluding a law enforcement officer during a high speed chase. I hereby sentence you to six months probation, forty hours of community service and restitution in the amount of $1,000. Also, you are only permitted to operate a motor vehicle for the express purpose of employment. Do I make myself clear?"

"Yes, your honor, you make yourself clear."

My father dropped his head as if he could not believe that his daughter was in this predicament.

The $1,000 restitution was to be paid to the movie theater to cover the insurance deductible they had to pay to their insurance company. The cars damaged, mine and the cab that I ran into, were covered by my insurance company. Of course, this caused them to raise my rates to an outrageous amount. How in the world was I going to pay the $1,000 restitution, the new insurance rate, as well as my regular living expenses, on a maid's salary?

I thought I would be making decent money since I had a college degree, but I was not able to find a professional job. And now I was declared a convicted felon. That sure will not go in my favor as far as landing a professional position. Once again, Aunt Rose came to my rescue and let me move in with her to save money so that I could meet my legal financial obligations—$1,000 restitution plus monthly probationary fees.

I believe she also wanted me to move in with her so that she could watch over me and impart some of her wisdom to me. Aunt Rose was full of life lessons. She gave out lots of good advice and never passed judgment on me. My parents had offered to let me move back home, but I knew it came with a price— constant putdowns by my father. My mother did not condemn me the way my father did, but she seldom came to my rescue when my father started on his tirades about how I was never going to amount to anything.

There it is again! That same question. Why, oh why, is that same question on most job applications? Have you ever being convicted of a felony or first degree misdemeanor? The answer to that question certainly does not increase my chances of getting a job. That has no bearing on whether or not I can do the jobs I am applying for. Why must I be defined by my past? I paid my dues for the dumb mistake I made, so why can't I move on with my life and not be hindered by one bad move, one bad night. I am not a bad person. I just made a few wrong decisions.

I am quite frustrated with my life. I have a bachelors' degree in social work, but since I graduated from college three years ago, I have not been able to find a job in my field or any job that required a degree. For the last three years, I have been a maid at Bob's Motel. Don't get it twisted—I was one of the best maids there. In fact, the manager often told me that he could see me as a manager in the future. *This is not what I had in mind when I said I wanted a job helping people. I'm helping people all right. I'm just not helping myself very much.*

I found it quite a drag, day after day, cleaning rooms of people who, for the most part, appeared to be enjoying life. On the occasions I saw the people who occupied the rooms, I thought, *I'd rather be in your shoes than mine.* I often found myself daydreaming, imagining what types of lives these people led. I often fantasized about a tall, dark, handsome, rich man coming to my rescue and taking me home to be his wife. Then it would not bother me to clean up behind others . . . my husband and the children we would have someday.

Carla, my classmate who returned home to Tampa, Florida, called me one day. "Hi, Lissy. Have you found a job yet?"

"Not really. No one seems to be hiring." *At least they are not hiring felons,* I thought. "I've searched high and low, but no one seems to want me."

"Well, why don't you send me your resume and I'll pass it along to my brother to see if he can find you a job here at the hospital. I'll tell him what a good person you are and how you motivated me to finish college."

I had been in touch with Carla a few times since we graduated, but I never told her what happened that night after we celebrated our graduation or the consequences of my actions. *If only you knew, you probably would avoid me like the plague the way employers do.* I was in quite a quandary. Should I tell Carla about my situation or just send her my resume and hope that I can land a job in spite of my background? Aunt Rose often told me, "Nothing risked, nothing gained." I had a lot to risk and possibly a lot to gain, so I sent my resume and hoped for the best. The worst that could happen was that Carla would know about my record and desert me like most of my friends had and I wouldn't get the job. Well, I decided it was worth the risk, so I sent my resume to her in Tampa.

Two weeks went by with no word from Carla. *Just as I figured, they did a background check on me and won't hire me because of my record.* I was about to give up on the possibility of a job in Tampa when Carla called me.

"Lissy, I have good news for you. At least I hope it is good news."

My heart was pounding and Carla could not tell me her thoughts quick enough. "Okay, friend, let's hear it."

Carla took a deep breath before continuing. "There is a lady at my church who just received a grant from MADD—Mothers Against Drunk Drivers. She needs someone to be a spokesperson: give motivational speeches to schools and teen organizations. I was thinking you might be a good candidate. I hope you don't mind that I did a little research before I shared your resume with her."

I was quite embarrassed, but being embarrassed was becoming a part of who I was. "I'm okay with that."

"Great. I'll have Mrs. Washington call you to set up an interview. Keep the faith. I believe there are great things in store for you here in Tampa."

Lissy fell to her knees. "Lord, I thank you for where you are taking me. I stand on your word in Jeremiah 29:1—*For I know the thoughts that I think toward you, saith the Lord, thoughts of peace, and not of evil, to give you an expected end.*

8. Wrong Turns, Irma Clark, ineclark@cs.com

9.

Country Girl, City Girl, Bad Girl

Jane Ann Keil-Stevens

She dropped the postcard in the corner mailbox, wishing she was going to the same place the card was. She tried not to let herself think of such things; especially those that weren't likely to happen anytime soon. Even a simple gesture like mailing a card back home to Iowa was enough to make her long for the comfort of her family and the simple but secure life she led there. That was no longer possible, considering what she had done. Her only choice was to make the best of it, but that didn't mean that Lisette ("Lissy" to her family and friends) Donavan had to like it.

Living in New York City after spending her whole life in the sleepy little town of Melville, Iowa, had been a major adjustment. She was managing fairly well on her own, considering the bizarre circumstances leading up to where she was now. Back home, she knew what she had intended to do was wrong, even if she was doing it for a good reason. Once the authorities heard the reason she did it, she was sure they would understand and go easy on her.

But that's not what happened. Her plan backfired and that's when all the trouble started. She'd had nightmares about it for weeks afterward. Now that the bad dreams had finally stopped, she wondered if they were coming true since she was living in a city with no family, no friends, and strangers who couldn't be trusted. She was one among many in a tough city where people didn't have that inward Iowa kindness about them; far from it. She was a square peg in a round hole; a misfit. It was up to her to find her way in her new surroundings, and no matter how hard she tried, she wasn't sure she could. Of course, she would frequently send postcards telling her family she was doing fine, even though that wasn't exactly true. She couldn't upset them any more than she already had. They worried about her being alone in a big city where she knew no one. For her situation, that was a good thing. For her parents' peace of mind, it was not.

Lissy was the kind of girl who played by the rules. She was the star pupil, the one who would do her homework on time, obeyed her parents, had dreams of being the first one in her family to graduate from college; and was torn between majoring in business or social work. Lissy didn't fit the stereotype of the middle child; she was too smart and too ambitious to be categorized that way.

Lissy's older brother, Ryan, managed a restaurant in her hometown. He never had any desire to go to college and was happy enough to remain in their little Midwest town. He lived a simple life, but for him, it was fine.

Shannon, Lissy's younger sister by three years, was the typical "good girl in a bad crowd" story. She had gotten pregnant a few years after high school and being a young, single mother with no education beyond that, the best she could do was work dead-end low-paying jobs. A few years later, she got pregnant again and now was caring for her six-year-old daughter and a three-year-old son. Lissy's parents volunteered to babysit if Shannon wanted to go to college, but she refused. She said she would provide for her kids on her own.

Lissy thought it noble of Shannon not to want to burden her parents, but Lissy worried that as the years went by, Shannon might not have another chance like that. Shannon was very headstrong and independent and wanted to manage it by herself. It broke Lissy's heart to see her sister in a position such as this and Lissy wanted to do everything she could to help her.

About a year ago, Lissy decided to take matters into her own hands. It was an unusually cold Iowa winter night and she went to visit Shannon and the kids. When she entered the rundown apartment in not the best of neighborhoods, she found the place freezing. She looked at her niece and nephew and saw their teeth chattering and their little fingers were cold as ice to her touch. They were huddled together on the threadbare couch wrapped in blankets and sitting in front of a space heater.

"Shannon, don't you know how dangerous it is to have a heater like that?"

"Yes, I know, but it's all I can afford right now. There is no way I can pay for something better at the moment."

"If you can't afford to keep the kids warm, then bring them to Mom and Dad's house. You know they wouldn't mind. Really. I hate to see them cold."

"I am not going there! I can take care of my own kids. I really don't need you on my back about it, too."

"I'm worried about all of you not being warm enough. The next thing you know, any or all of you will be in the hospital with pneumonia!"

"Thanks, but spare me the drama. We'll be fine. We have survived so far and we will make it through this until the weather gets warmer. I appreciate your concern, but we'll be ok."

Shannon had put herself and the kids in a really bad spot. Lissy noticed that the kids were wearing summer weight pajamas in the middle of winter with mounds of blankets around them. She felt bad for her sister, but worse for the kids. She knew they were suffering and she vowed to somehow help them. She didn't know how to make good on that promise—she just knew those kids weren't going to be cold for much longer. That's when the idea came to her. All she had to do was figure out how to pull it off without a hitch.

She didn't have to think about it too long before she came up with an idea that was really risky; yet, if it worked, Shannon and the kids would be warm and that was Lissy's only thought behind her plan. She couldn't let her niece and nephew suffer with no heat on these frigid Iowa nights. It was ridiculous to have Lissy know the three of them were freezing. She just had to do something to help them, whether Shannon wanted her to or not. Right then and there she made a mental list of what the kids needed: heavy socks, winter weight pajamas, slippers, and probably even winter coats. But the problem was that her own finances didn't make the A-list.

She was barely scraping by herself, and anything beyond the basics was nearly out of the question. If she could somehow manage to get the things they needed, the kids could keep warm at night and she wouldn't have to worry about them. Lissy knew she had to put a plan in place and she was a little afraid of what she kept coming up with. Her bank account wasn't all that healthy at the moment, so she only had one option: she would steal what the kids needed! Yeah, people did it all the time and got away with it. Why couldn't she do the same thing?

She thought about the idea for a long time. As she looked into her bedroom mirror brushing her auburn hair, she noticed that her hazel eyes were not as bright as they usually were. She figured it was due to the stress she was under, knowing what she was about to do was against the law and the punishment could be terrible, too. Yet, the thought of those adorable kids suffering like they were was more than she could take. She had devised a plan, she decided to follow through with it, and that was that.

On the outside, she was confident she could get the clothes for the kids with no problem, but on the inside, it was a different story. She started to have nightmares about it and getting a good night's sleep was a thing of the past. The longer she waited, the more nervous she got. So she decided the best route to take was to just get it over with and then she could relax. Every day she waited was another day of agony for the kids and she couldn't take that.

So, before she even had time to talk herself out of it, she calmly walked into Casey's Babies and Little Ones store to look at what they had. She'd been in this store a few times and knew the people who owned it. That's another reason this was so hard—she was planning to steal from people she knew and from people who had always been friendly and respectful to her. Is this how she was going to return that friendship, by stealing from them? All of a sudden, she realized how low she had sunk to even consider such a thing! It was too risky, too dangerous. Maybe she shouldn't do it, because part of her wanted to rush out of the store and just forget the whole thing. The other part of her wanted to do it for her niece and nephew. They needed her to do it.

Of course, her small town didn't offer a myriad of stores to choose from. At this very moment, she wished she was in a store where no one knew who she was. She told herself if that were the case, this whole thing would be a lot easier to pull off. She wondered if that was really true, but she didn't have time to dwell on it. It was time to get down to business. Now that she had committed herself to doing it, with the sole purpose of helping the kids, she was ready to get it over with.

She found some great things for her niece and nephew. A salesperson came up and asked, "Can I help you find something?"

"Oh no, thanks, I'm just looking." Yeah, sure. She was looking alright, but looking for something to steal and get safely out of the store with it. All of a sudden, her palms got sweaty, she felt like everyone was looking at her, which they weren't, and her cheeks turned tomato red. She could feel the resulting heat on her face. It was hard to ignore her discomfort, but then she remembered her niece and nephew and their discomfort. That thought alone was all she needed to spring into action, for the kids' sake.

She cleverly picked up a pair of heavyweight little girls' pajamas and other items the kids needed and walked around the store with them over her left arm. Up till now, she looked like any other shopper in the store. With a deep breath and a prayer, she quickly stuffed the items into her tote bag and managed to head toward the exit. So far, so good. Her eyes darted back and forth to see if anyone was looking at her in a suspicious way. Right now, everything looked surprisingly normal. No one was looking at her. The shoppers were browsing, Lissy was almost at the door and things were looking good. It was going according to plan and nothing seemed unusual.

She got to the front of the store and managed to open the heavy glass door and walk outside without anyone noticing what she had done. She did it! She didn't know if she was happy because she actually pulled it off or if she was disappointed in herself for what she had just done. For a moment, she was elated to know that no one had noticed. Nobody was chasing her and no one seemed to care that she had just walked out of the store with something she didn't pay for. Running would just give her away, so she walked at a brisk pace to her car, where she thought she would be safe and for now, she was.

Lissy passed by familiar streets she had known all her life, realizing today was different than any other day she had ever known. Today was the day she stole things from people she knew. She felt as if she were a marked woman with a terrible secret, a secret that was probably going to eat her alive. It didn't feel right. It was strange with the accompanying sick-to-her-stomach feeling. Lissy told herself it was nerves; after all, look what she had just done!

She pulled into the driveway of her parents' home, got out of the car and walked in the house as if nothing happened. The truth of the matter was that there was something wrong, something was very wrong.

Lissy dropped down on her bed, thankful that it had worked out the way it did. She was relieved, but at the same time, she realized that she would probably always be looking over her shoulder. But she would worry about that later; for now, she could relax as best she could. Her heart was still racing, and she decided to take an aspirin and put her feet up. She felt as if she was behaving strangely, even though she wasn't. It was more like her insides were in such a panic that her whole being was off kilter. She eased herself squarely on the bed and desperately tried to block out what had just happened.

Just then, the doorbell rang. She jumped off the bed as she strained to hear the conversation that was going on at the front door.

"Mrs. Donavan?"

"Yes, that's me."

"Do you have a daughter, Lisette, living here?"

"Wait a minute. What is this all about and why are you asking questions about my daughter?

"We are here to inform her that she is under arrest."

Lissy heard no more as she snuck out the back door. She took off running with a vengeance. Her heart was beating wildly in her chest as she ran. Her legs were about to give out as she ran through neighbors' backyards. She was running for her life, literally, and when she had run for about five blocks, she stopped to catch her breath. There was no energy left, she had exhausted it all. She had no idea where she was going, but the one thing she did know is that she was never going back home again.

She managed to run in the direction of her best friend's house and she ran to the front door. Luckily, Jenny answered.

"Lissy, you look terrible, what is it? Why is your face so red? Why are you out of breath?"

"I can't tell you that right now. I'm in a bad spot, and I need to borrow some money. I'll pay it back, I swear."

"I'm not worried about that. I just want to know what's going on."

"I can't tell you right now. I will when things settle down, I promise. But for now, I just need some money, please. I'll explain everything later."

"Ok, well, I just cashed my check and I have $300, but that's all I can give you."

"That would be great! With the little I have, that will be perfect!"

Jenny reluctantly handed Lissy the money, not knowing if she was doing the right thing or not. All she knew was that whatever was wrong, Lissy couldn't tell her about it, and for now, that would have to be enough.

Lissy took the money, flew out the door, looked back at Jenny, waved and continued to run.

When the airplane touched down, Lissy heard the announcement, "Welcome to New York City." For the first time in many hours, Lissy breathed a sigh of relief. She was safe, at least for now, but who knew how long that was going to last.

9. Country Girl, City Girl, Bad Girl, Jane Ann Keil-Stevens,
    jast820@comcast.net

10.

Family Ties

Shay Shoats

"No!!!" Lisette screamed while leaping up from her bed, swinging her arms wildly. Beads of sweat formed across her forehead in desperate attempts to catch her breath. She looked around her room, only to realize who she had been fighting was none other than Main Stray's sheets, wrapped around her like a snake. She leaned against the closet door and sighed in relief, only to be startled by rapid banging on the door. She jumped and sucked in a small sharp breath.

Then she heard a familiar voice calling. "Lissy! Lissy! Are you alright? Lissy! Lissy! Gurl, you better open up this damn door before I knock it down," the voice warned.

Lisette looked around the room again to discover this was not her bedroom in Jamaica, although it was similar. It was then that she realized that she was in the apartment of her former classmate from college, Najee. She knew she'd better hurry to the door because Najee was a woman of her word, and if she said she was going to knock the door down, then the door was coming down.

"Coming!" she said, as she tripped over her sheets rushing to the door. She began to hear Najee counting. Scrambling to turn the knob as Najee reached three, Lisette found herself once again trying to catch her breath. Still on the floor, Lisette shifted her body off her knees and sat on the floor. Exhausted she sighed again.

"Dang, girl, what's all that noise in here, and why you looked like you've been jumped?" Najee asked. Chuckling at her friend, Najee's smile quickly faded when she noticed Lisette was not joining her. "Lissy, what's wrong?" Najee asked, truly concerned about her friend.

Now controlling her breathing, Lisette looked up at her friend of ten years. *"Should I tell her?"* she thought. *"Should I tell her about the nightmares that haunt me almost every night; about how paranoid I am when I walk down the street; about the money I stole to get to the U.S. to hide me from my father's wrath? More importantly, should I tell Najee that her once outgoing, energetic, fun loving friend was gone, and she now housed a murderer?"*

"I'm fine," Lisette said. She got up off the hardwood floor and began to get ready for work. She looked in the mirror with a tear in her eye. *"Where has the time gone?"* she mumbled to herself.

Little Lisette Donavan grew up in a house that most people would call a mansion, especially in Jamaica where the cost of living is cheaper. From the age of five, she had a full staff waiting on her hand and foot. Lisette, being the spoiled little girl she was, tortured the poor servants by throwing her clean clothes on the floor and trample them until they became dirty again. She would also take paint and scribble all over the white walls and floors because she knew the maids were not allowed to lay a finger on her.

Lisette never received any discipline from her father regarding her behavior. Her father, Nicardo Donavan, a drug lord in Jamaica, held the maids responsible for the house—if anything was out of place, they suffered the consequences. No one wanted to face the wrath of Mr. Donavan. His temper was legendary. Once, a young gardener accidentally cut down the rose bush in the center of Mr. Donavan's garden; a rose bush that he'd named Rosetta and highly favored. The young gardener ran to Nicardo explaining the accident and pleading for his forgiveness. Nircardo chained the boy up in his stable and beat him profusely with a whip for eight days, allowing the maids to only give him water and a slice of bread each day. This event quickly became known as the Eight Days of Terror.

Now, getting out of the cab and looking up at the five-star hotel where she worked, Lisette found a new respect for her father's maids. She had only been back in the U.S. for two weeks, working as a maid only one week, but it already seemed like forever. She looked over at Najee with her navy blue and white pinstripe pantsuit and navy blue peep toe slingbacks. Her dreads were pulled back in a neat little bun. She carried her purse on her shoulder and briefcase in her hand. Standing at five-eleven, with a size four frame, Najee looked like the executive business manager she was. Lisette smiled at her friend, but couldn't hide the pain she felt as she looked down at her maid's uniform—thick pantyhose with white orthopedic-looking shoes. Her silky straight hair was also pulled back in a bun. Even though the uniform was dated, her size eight figure, along with a few alterations, made the ensemble appear chic. Since Najee was taller and slimmer, wearing a DKNY suit automatically commanded attention. Lisette's curves, which were in all the right places, still managed to turn heads.

Lisette didn't care about the heads she turned. She recalled Najee and she both going to school for business management. Ironically, it was her idea they minor in hotel management. Yet, when they walked into the lovely establishment, they headed in separate directions—Najee to her office and Lisette to the top floor to join her supervisor, Laurel, to finish her last day of housekeeping training. The elevator chimed and the doors opened onto several luxury suites. Lisette found Laurel starting her day off in the Presidential Suite. She was troubled by the fumes coming from the suite. The smells of vomit, alcohol, and urine filled the air. She entered the room and quickly covered her mouth and nose in an attempt to mask the stench.

"OMG! What happened in here?" Lisette asked loudly, not wanting to step any further.

"Oh, child, this ain't nothing. Just some young spoiled little college kids acting up," Laurel answered, clearly unaffected by the smells and scene.

Lisette watched the older woman who was in her 60's but could easily pass for someone in her 40's. Mrs. Laurel, from Alabama, gathered up empty beer bottles, dirty undergarments, and

The 21 Lives of Lisette Donavan   87

empty condom wrappers with her latex gloves. Lisette finally got up enough nerve to go in and help the woman. As she poured a powdered chemical on the spots where vomit remained on the carpet, tears began to form in her eyes. Lisette's mood began to change to that of hopelessness.

"I can't do this," she said to herself in a low whisper.

Laurel still heard her new employee and felt bad for her. She usually didn't care about the bourgeoisie types, but there was something about Lisette that was different. She was growing fond of the pretty girl, but she could tell Lisette was a fish out of water.

"I know what we need," Laurel said as she jumped up from resting her feet. "Some music," she announced, as she walked over to a small radio and began to search for a good station. She stopped and turned up the volume when she heard Freddie Jackson singing, *Rock Me Tonight*. "WHOA!!!" she screamed. "That's my song!" she exclaimed as she began to sway her hips from side to side with her arms in the air doing the same. Lisette stared at her supervisor for a moment in disbelief, before letting a chuckle escape her lips. "Oh, you young kids don't know nothing 'bout real music," she said as she ignored Lisette and continued dancing.

"Yes, I do." Lisette defended herself and jumped up to join her. The women continued their day cleaning each suite with the little radio playing everything from Arthur Conley's *Sweet Soul Music*, to Stevie Wonder's *All I do*, and Earth, Wind, and Fire's *Boogie Wonderland*. The day flew by and before they knew it, it was already the end of their shift. After clocking out and grabbing her things, Lisette found herself waiting in the bar area for Najee to finish her work. Sitting alone with nothing but her thoughts, Lisette felt her sadness begin to rear its ugly head.

"Lissy," a male voice called in a thick Jamaican accent. Lisette froze. She knew only her friends and family called her by that name. "Lissy Donavan," the man spoke louder.

She slowly turned around to find her childhood friend, Dimarche, standing not even five feet from her.

"Hi," she said slowly. She was happy to see a familiar face but, at the same time, she was completely terrified. *Oh, no,* she thought. *How much did he know? What did he know, if he knew anything? Why was he here? How did he find me?*

She was engrossed in her thoughts until she heard him say, "Hey, stranger, long time no see." He smiled at her while approaching with his arms open. She slowly got up from the stool and allowed him to envelope her fully. Her body tensed, but quickly relaxed as his wide, well cut chest covered hers. His muscular arms wrapped around her body like a warm firm blanket, and if that wasn't bad enough, the smell of Cool Water cologne filled her nose. *Damn, and he smells good too*, she thought. *I'm in trouble now*. She tried to pull away, but he remained, holding her a few seconds longer than he should have. When he finally let her go, she looked him in his eyes and immediately became heated with desire.

She hadn't seen him since she'd left for college. Back then he was a goofy little boy with a big head and extra thin body, whom she secretly nicknamed Lollipop. Now he'd grown up to about six-two, weighing about 225 pounds with no fat anywhere.

"Lolli—I mean Dimarche!" she said trying to hide the lust in her eyes. He smiled at her again. Just then, Najee walked in and interrupted the reunion by announcing she was done. Lisette quickly introduced them and told Dimarche she had to go. After a few pleas and puppy dog faces, she agreed to stay a little longer to catch up on old times. "I'll see her home safe and sound myself. I promise," Dimarche assured Najee.

Najee left reluctantly. Lisette and Dimarche sat down at a nearby table. They spent the next five hours eating and having a few drinks. They reminisced of old times and even enjoyed a few quiet moments where they stared into each other's eyes. Lisette couldn't fight the attraction she felt. Dimarche was fine, but more importantly, they had a genuine connection.

"I think I better get you home," he said looking at the clock to find it was 11:00 P.M.

"So soon?" She was doing the complaining now.

He couldn't help laughing at the role reversal. "Yes, you have to work tomorrow, and I promised Najee I'd see you home," he said, standing up and reaching for her hand. They paid the tab and caught a cab. After they got in the cab, their levels of desire increased significantly. They began kissing and touching to the point that if they were anywhere else they would be making love. The cab driver interrupted the heat of the moment by clearing his throat and informing them that they had arrived at their destination. They both looked up as if the reality set in that their fantasy was over.

Dimarche paid the driver plus a tip to hold the ride while he walked Lisette to the door. They got out of the vehicle holding hands and strolling to the door. "You know you can stay the night," she offered.

He looked at her, smiled, and said, "No I have to go check in," he said, backing away from her.

She pulled him back to her and said, "So check in tomorrow." She kissed his lips lightly.

"I can't," he said as he embraced her once more. "Then your father will be looking for both of us."

Lisette's mouth dropped. She couldn't believe her ears. "I . . . I gotta go," she managed to say before she unlocked the door and rushed inside.

Lisette was greeted by the morning sun and the birds singing. Although it was a beautiful day outside, the reality and horror of last night's turn of events crept back into her mind.

"He works for my father," she uttered aloud. Still in disbelief, she pulled the covers over her head in an attempt to go back to sleep when there was a knock on her door.

Before she could tell the person to go away, Najee opened the door. "Lissy, Dimarche is here to see you, and he brought breakfast," she beamed.

Lisette threw back the covers and jumped up. "He's here, now?" she asked urgently.

"Yes," Najee said, smiling but not recognizing the panic in Lisette's voice.

Lisette quickly threw on an oversized tee shirt and a pair of jogging pants and rushed passed Najee.

"What are you doing here?" she asked, walking into the kitchen while Dimarche was taking fresh bagels and cream cheese out of the paper bag.

"Serving you breakfast," he replied calmly. "We need to talk," he added.

"Oh, yeah, well, I don't," she said flatly.

"Lissy, come on," he said, pausing to see how serious she was.

Najee walked into the kitchen. Hearing her friend being difficult, she said, "Lissy, the man brought breakfast. The least you can do is eat and listen to him." She then grabbed a bagel and a small container of cream cheese and walked back into her bedroom.

"So this was all a job for you? To seduce me back to Jamaica so my father can deal with me?" she asked accusingly.

"No, my job was to bring you home period, but I love you and that complicates things," he sighed.

"You love me?" she asked.

"Since we were kids," he admitted. "I want to help you, but you have to tell me what happened the night you fled the country," he said seriously. Lisette knew it was time to come clean.

She began explaining the argument her stepmom and she had. Her stepmom didn't want Lissy to come around because she weakened her father's power. Then, her stepmom suddenly pulled a gun on her. In the heat of the moment, Lissy dove for the gun. It went off, leaving her stepmom in a puddle of her own blood. "I panicked, so I went into my father's safe, stole his money, ran home, grabbed a few things, and caught a plane to New York."

He sat and listened to Lisette intensely. "Wow!" was all he could say.

She shrugged her shoulders, "So what does he want you to do with me?" she asked nervously.

Instead of answering her, he asked, "What do you think? Do you want to go back?"

"No, I think I'm done with my dad's lifestyle, his status, and with Jamaica, period. I just want to start all over again.

"Then, that's what we'll do," he said. "Now go pack your bags."

She looked at him curiously. "What?" she asked.

"We can't start over here, so I was thinking Paris is good for a nice start."

She squealed in excitement, then ran to gather her things.

As she entered her bedroom Dimarche's cell phone began to ring. "Yo," he said.

"Have you found her yet?" a male's voice asked.

"No," he answered.

"Look, don't play with me. She was supposed to kill my wife and take the fall. She can't take the fall if she's not here," Nicardo said.

"I can't believe you would do that to your own daughter, your family," Dimarche said, shaking his head.

"Family is family. This is business, and I need to get the cops off my back. Until I get this major deal done, sacrifices have to be made," he said with a smirk. "You just find her quick, and I'll throw in another $25,000 to add to your $75,000."

Dimarche smiled. "All right, I'll call you back later," he said, staring at Lisette, looking as beautiful as ever in her red and white sundress, red hat, shoes, and sunglasses to match.

"Ok, I'm ready," she said. She told Najee the plan and that she'd call her later to fill her in. Dimarche loaded up the cab he called and they were all saying their goodbyes. Dimarche got to the car, then stopped.

"Hold on," he said, as Lisette got into the car. He turned around, reached into his pocket, pulled out his cell phone, broke it in half, and threw it in the dumpster on the side of the road.

"Ok, let's go," he said, and the cab driver pulled off. They arrived at the airport and booked their flight. Shortly afterward they were on the airplane.

"I'll be right back," Dimarche said, heading toward the restroom. The flight attendant instructed everyone to turn off their cell phones.

Lisette opened her purse and pulled out her cell, but before she could turn it off, a text came through stating, "Plan B, you know what to do?"

She quickly responded. "Yes, Daddy," then turned her cell off.

10. Family Ties, Shay Shoats, KBShoats@gmail.com

11.

A Voice of MY Own

Anita L. Gray

"Hello. Yes, this is Lisette Donavan."

"Ms. Donavan, this is Mr. Rowe from Jae's Studios. We would like to invite you to our final casting call for the up and coming Broadway play, *My Lies Are True.* On Wednesday, we will provide you a list of songs from the play. Everyone will have one hour to learn one song and perform it in front of our private investors and sponsors."

"Great, Mr. Rowe. Yes, I would love to attend. I look forward to seeing you Wednesday. Thank you, goodbye." As she hung up with Mr. Rowe, Lisette couldn't help but rejoice out loud. "Oh thank you, Father Lord. Finally a job where I can use my music degree! Ms. Pierce will be glad to hear those expensive voice lessons are starting to pay off. Now, if I can just make it to 125th Street! Ugh, I hate Harlem rush hour traffic. Mrs. Pierce will have my head on a platter if I'm late again! Get out of the road! Some people have jobs to get to!"

"Lissy, is that you?"

"Yes, Ma'am, Mrs. Pierce, it's me."

"I was starting to worry about you, baby. I thought something awful happened to you. These streets of New York aren't safe for a beautiful, colored girl like yourself."

"I'm so sorry for being late, Ma'am. I got a final call back today! Mr. Rowe from Jae's Studios invited me to perform one song Wednesday to see if I will be cast in a new play coming to Broadway. I have never been so excited and nervous in my whole life."

"Come now, hurry child. It's past time for my bath, and sing me one of those beautiful songs my money is paying for. Walking around all alone in this big ole brownstone has me feeling a bit tired. Call back, you say. Broadway play for colored singers. My, how things have changed. Lisette Donavan, before your mama died, I told her to talk to you about those big dreams you seem to always talk about. Broadway is no place for a colored girl, no matter how beautiful you are. Your mother had the voice of an angel. Oh, how she would sing so sweetly around this house while she cooked and cleaned. I knew you would be able to sing just as well because you have her beauty. Lissy, help me to my room. I need my bed. I feel sleep all over me."

"Now, Mrs. Pierce, that is quite enough chatter for one evening."

"Jason Pierce, how long have you been in this room?"

"Hello, Lissy. Long enough to know that you are late again. You have big hopes and dreams my mother seems to think you will never be able to fulfill, although she believes so much in your abilities to sing she is paying for you to take lessons."

"Shhh! Get out. Get out right now Jason. She's asleep."

"Why are you so upset with me, beautiful Lissy? I didn't refer to you as a colored girl, although your beautiful cocoa skin, curvy hips, sexy lips, and alluring big brown eyes have called to me ever since we were kids."

"When did you get in town, and why are you here? You didn't even speak up and let your mother know you were in the room?"

"Well, I have a business meeting on Wednesday, so I flew in this morning. Congrats on your final casting call. I know you will get the starring role with that beautiful voice of yours."

"Hmm, it must be nice to fly in and out of town for meetings. How did you know about my casting call? After four long years at New York State and voice lessons, courtesy of your mother, I am just now landing my first real shot at my dream job. I have always wanted to sing in front of thousands and thousands of people. Do you remember how we use to sit on the steps of this house, and I would put on a concert for you?"

"Yes, your big head had those big chestnut curls bouncing up and down singing the jazzy sounds of Rochelle Ferrell. I will never forget, Lissy. Have dinner with me tomorrow night?"

"Ha, no thank you, Mr. Pierce! I have to clean your mother's house and practice for Wednesday. I have to get a good part. I really need the money."

"It's only dinner. You have to eat. Bring the twins, Kaylan and Clarke."

"Thank you, but no thank you. Our parents didn't raise us to take charity. The only reason I even work for your mother is because I promised my mother I would see about Mrs. Pierce when you ran off to see the world. So, excuse me. I have work to do."

"Hello, I'm home! Kaylan? Clarke? Where are you guys? I have some wonderful news. You will never guess what happened to me today? Why isn't this kitchen clean?"

"Why are you yelling, Lisette Donavan?"

"Kaylan, didn't I ask you all to get this place clean before I came home?"

"Oh, what for? You finally have a hot date?"

"No, just a few friends for dinner tomorrow night, so help me get this place clean. Where is Clarke?"

"He and his latest girlfriend left today for Chicago. He said to tell you he would call when he got there safe, and he loves you and will see you next week."

"Huh. It's so hard to see my little twins so grown now."

"Yeah, whatever, Lissy. You always said you couldn't wait 'til we were old enough to take care of ourselves so you didn't have to worry about what we ate, where we slept or who we talked to. Man, I used to think if Ma and Dad could hear some of the mean and cruel things you said to us, they would jump out that cold ground and slap the black off yah!"

"Look, you were too young to understand the pressure I felt when they died. I had to do some things I'm not proud of just to keep a roof over our heads, clothes on our backs, and food on the table."

"Whatever, Lisette. You know Jason's mother always helped us when we needed anything. Ma worked for that crazy 'ole lady all her life, and when dad was killed, she really took us in. You were just plain wild. I remember Mrs. Pierce having to come get you from jail many times. I never understood why you always managed to end up in jail just when she would have bought us the nicest clothes and brought all of our favorite foods to the house. I hated you for making Mrs. Pierce's life so hard. Yes, she can be a bit weird, but I just think since her mind isn't quite right. She sometimes forgets that it isn't 1950."

"Look Ms. Know Nothing, I never liked jail, and Mrs. Pierce didn't start helping us out until I agreed to take Ma's place and work for her as her maid! Yes, she is a sweet old lady, but I was the one that took care of you and Clarke. Me! The only reason I went to jail was I got caught stealing trying to make sure you all had everything you needed and some of the things you wrote to Santa Claus for Christmas. I worked and put myself through school until I got that scholarship Jason told me about our freshman year of college. So, excuse me if the only memories you have of your big sister is of me behind bars. I did what I had to for you and Clarke. Now get this place clean."

"Um, why didn't you ever tell us, Lissy? Why make us believe Mrs. Pierce was taking care of us all these years? I am so sorry. I love you so much, Lissy. Look, you said you had some good news today—what happened?"

"I got a call back for *My Lies Are True.* Not that you care, just get this house clean. I have to get to East Bronx for my voice lessons with Ms. Parker."

"Do, re, mi, fa, so, la, ti, do.
        "Again, with feeling."
        "Do, re, mi, fa, so, la, ti, do."
        "Lisette, you sound great. Just watch your pitch and try not to be so airy on the higher notes. I know you will land a great part in this play."

"Thank you so much, Ms. Parker. I will keep that in mind. I am so nervous, but I think I am ready."

"So how is everything going? Is Mrs. Pierce doing any better? I just can't see how you stand her when she thinks it is still 1950. That colored girl thing would really get on my nerves. I hear Jason is back with his fine, rich self."

"Ms. Parker, you are a mess. Yes, he is back, and no, she doesn't bother me. She's harmless."

"Umm, I didn't hear you dispute me about how cute Jason is. So, you do think he is attractive, don't you?"

"I haven't really noticed. We kind of grew up together, but we are from two different worlds. His family is rich, and he has been given life on a silver spoon. My mother had to work really hard to take care of him and his family. He is a really nice guy, but we are only friends because my mother made him act nice to me when we were kids."

"Lisette, he isn't married and you don't have a man. I know he has noticed how beautiful you are, and you are going to be a very successful singer and songwriter one day. Isn't he some type of hot shot producer or play writer or something?"

"Honestly, I'm not too sure what all he does. He always travels, and we talk about investments and things like that. He never seemed to be that interested in coming to see me in any of my plays."

"Well, Lisette, have you ever invited him to come see you?"

"Umm, come to think about it, no. After all these years, I never once thought to ask him if he would be willing to come and see anything I was in. Besides, he is so busy and in and out of town. I don't think he would make time for me, although he did ask me to dinner last night."

"And what did you say?"

"Well, I said no because I have a friend coming over for dinner tonight."

"Look, Lisette, you have been taking lessons from me for the last two years. I know you are a wonderful person and he comes from a really wonderful family. The Pierce family raised money to buy the Boys and Girls Club downtown. His family is well known in this community, and they have wonderful connections. I don't think it would hurt you to be nice to him. Why not invite him over? He is your friend, right? You have never had anything negative to say about him, so just loosen up a little. You never know where love lies."

"I will try to keep that in mind. I've got to run home. Thanks again, Ms. Parker.

"Get the door, Kaylan."

"Okay. Tina is here, Lissy"

"Hey diva, come on in. Tina, you are looking so good. I love your new hair cut. It is so cute.

"Thank you girl, I went to that new spot on 5th Avenue. You know, Tony knows how to hook a sister up with a short cut.

"Lissy, where is the wine? I love what you have done with this place. Kaylan is getting so grown and tall. Clarke and she are how old now?"

"Girl, they are twenty-one years old. Can you believe it? The wine is in the cooler, Tina."

"Wow, time is really going by. I am starting to feel a bit old. I guess it is about time for me to get married. Doug proposed!"

"Wow! Tina, I am so happy for you and Doug. Pour the wine while I see who is at the door."

"Hello, beautiful."

"Jason, what are you doing here?"

"If I recall, I asked you to dinner last night."

"Yes, you did, and I recall telling you no."

"Well, I thought I would drop over to see if I could persuade you to reconsider my offer."

"Lissy, girl, go throw on that sexy black dress you just bought last week and go out with Jason. I am leaving."

"Tina, you just got here. What about our plans? What about this dinner I just made?"

"Lissy, I just came by to show off my ring. You better start working on one of your own. I wasn't going to eat your food. You know you can't cook."

"Whatever, Tina. Get out. I might call you tomorrow after I leave my casting call."

"Bye, girl. Call me with all the juicy details. And Jason, make sure you show her a good time. She needs it. It's been awhile since she has been on a date."

"Well, Mr. Pierce, it appears I am saying yes. It will only take me about ten minutes to change."

"Hurry up and back out already so I can park. Ugh! I am so glad Jae's Studio has covered garage parking."

"Good morning, ladies. Today is going to be very exciting, stressful, and fun. My name is Mr. Rowe of Jae's Studios, and we are looking for one of you to star in my up and coming Broadway play, *My Lies Are True*. I hope you got your rest last night and are coming to work hard and put on a good show for my investors and sponsors. We have been to Los Angeles, Atlanta, and now we are here in New York City. You are the final twenty young ladies we feel will fit the part we are looking to cast. Some of our investors and sponsors wish to keep their identities secret; therefore, you will be singing in front of a two-way mirror one hour from now. Please follow my assistant to the next room to learn the song you will be performing."

"Mr. Pierce, can I get you a drink before you go into the viewing room, sir?

"No, I am fine. Wait, I am feeling a bit out of sorts. I got in late last night. Bring me a bottle of spring water."

"Yes sir, right away."

"Mr. Pierce, I would like to thank you for flying in to personally pick out our cast for this play. I know you are a busy man, and we consider it an honor for you to be here with us today."

"I am glad to hear it, Mr. Rowe. My partners have really spoken highly of your studio and I am a man who enjoys an angelic voice and beauty as well as the next man. I will be investing almost two million dollars to help with this play, so it is very important I oversee the star roles. We must have just the right face and voice for these parts."

"Yes sir, I agree. It's just that you have invested in so many other plays in the past and you never came to a final casting call. I just wanted you to know it is a great honor to have you here."

"Well, my flight leaves in four hours, so let's bring these ladies out."

"Yes sir, Mr. Pierce, right away."

"Well, Mr. Pierce, we are almost to the last young lady. We were hoping that you would pick at least three or four ladies and then we could narrow down the final part."

"I don't think I have heard the right voice yet. How many more have to sing?"

"Well, sir, we only have one more singer left."

"Well, what are we waiting for? Bring her on."

"Number twenty, Ms. Lisette Donavan. Front and center, please. You will have forty-five seconds to wow us. So what song will you be singing for us today?"

"I'm singing, *What Kind of Fool Am I,* by ALG.

What kind of fool am I, not to believe in love? What kind of fool couldn't see you standing there loving me. What kind of fool, rejects her own heart, blinded by what she feels could never be? What kind of fool am I? What kind of fool am I to make you love me?

"Excellent, thank you, Ms. Donavan. Someone will be contacting you by the end of next week."

"Thank you so much. I look forward to your call, Mr. Rowe."

"Mr. Rowe, she is the one I want for the starring role. Pay her $2,000.00 per show and allow her to pick her own personal stylist."

"Her own stylist, Mr. Pierce? Two-thousand dollars per show? We have never paid any singer that amount of money for any of our shows and no one ever got to pick their stylist."

"Look, Mr. Rowe, I am willing to invest a large sum of money into this godforsaken play of yours, but only if you hire Ms. Lisette Donavan on my terms!"

"Yes sir, I will make the call right now."

"Hello. Yes, this is Lisette Donavan. Yes, I would love to! Thank you so much Mr. Rowe, I won't let you down. Goodbye. Oh thank you Father Lord, finally a voice of my own. Lord, I have worked so hard for so long. Ma, Dad, I love you. Thank you so much for looking out for us. I made it! I am going to be a star on Broadway! Who should I call first?"

"Hello, Jason. Guess what?"

11. A Voice of MY Own, Anita L. Gray,
    neeterlrg@gmail.com

12.

In Due Time

Erica Belcher

"Well, well, well. If it isn't Miss Lisette Donavan and Mr. James Hugh," Calvin said in a mocking tone. "Say James, how'd you enjoy that game? I think it went fairly well, don't you? I guess I'll be seeing you real soon, huh, James?" Calvin snickered and walked away.

James and I were leaving a campus basketball game. He had just lost some money to Calvin because the team James bet on had lost. This meant that he was in one of his moods. This also meant that I could end up being his punching bag if I did not tread lightly. I was desperately trying to find something to take his mind off his loss.

"Do you want to get something to eat?" I asked.

"Oh, so I guess you're just going to rub it in that I don't have any money by suggesting that we go buy something to eat, huh?" he sharply replied.

I made sure to correct myself and said, "I meant that we can go to my place, and I can cook us something to eat."

This seemed to ease his mind, and I was grateful. I was also fooled. Once we got to my place, he lashed out immediately.

"So, I guess that was your way of trying to embarrass me. First, you ask to eat out when you know I just lost money, and then you say that we can eat at your house like I'm some broke Joe!"

The fear that arose in me each time he lashed out on me began to escalate. But this time, I was less afraid of being hit than I was angry. For years, I accepted the fact that the abuse was brought on by something I said or did. Strangely, I didn't feel that way this particular night. I felt that he was an absolute lunatic who constantly put himself into risky situations and then took his frustrations out on me when he lost at his gambles. I didn't feel like being his punching bag anymore.

"Do you hear me talking to you, you stupid bitch?" James screamed at the top of his lungs. And then the first blow came. I immediately saw stars. Without taking into account the fact that I was only five-five and 135 pounds versus his five-eleven, 260 pound frame, he continued to throw blows at me forcefully. When I tried to guard my face, he pushed me down. When I tried to get my balance, he'd start hitting me in the face again. I felt my whole face swell up. I also heard cracking noises and felt pangs all over. As James hit me another time, I tried to catch my balance on the kitchen counter. It was then that I saw a blurred object that turned out to be a steak knife. Before I knew it, I grabbed the knife. James struck me again. Everything went dark.

"Hello, anyone there?" a voice said, interrupting my thoughts.

"Yes," I replied.

"Hi, I'm Iris, the new cleaning assistant. I was told by Mr. Lee that I should meet you here so that you can teach me the ropes," she said with a broad and friendly smile.

"Hi, Iris, I'm Lisette. It's nice to meet you. Mr. Lee told me to expect you. Let me show you around."

Iris began to make small talk, and though I'm not one for small talk, I was ready to focus my attention on anything other than what I was just thinking about. Reliving that five-year-old nightmare was not on the top of my "to do" list.

"Are you married? Do you have children? How long have you been here?" Iris was shooting the questions out at the speed of lightning.

"No, I'm not married. I don't have children and I have been here for four years. How about you?" I asked.

"I'm still in college, undergrad, and need a part time job to have a little change in my pocket, you know?"

"Yeah, I remember those days," I replied.

"You went to college?" Iris asked, as if she were surprised.

"Yes, I graduated with my Bachelors of Science in Social Work. I started grad school but didn't finish. Other things came up," I explained. There was no way I was going to elaborate and tell her that I didn't finish because of what happened between James and me.

Iris hesitantly asked the next question. "If you have a B.S. in Social Work, why do you work here?"

I decided it was time to end the Q and A with Miss Iris and focus more on showing her the way around. Instead of answering her question, I said, "This is where we keep all of our cleaning supplies," and pointed to the cleaning supply closet. I continued to ignore her question as I showed her where everything was kept and how to properly clean everything. I noticed that she was a fast learner and was taking everything in quickly. I was grateful because the last woman in her position was a slow learner and just plain lazy. Instead of being a help, she actually created more work for me because I had to clean up behind her. I didn't expect this to be the case with Iris because after paying close attention to what I showed her, she got to work immediately.

As I left work that night, I remembered when I used to be the ambitious, young lady that Iris was. I began to wonder what happened to me. The realization that I was almost thirty (twenty-eight to be exact), had no kids, worked as a maid, and had very few to no friends was sinking in hard. I also realized that, even though I was considered an attractive woman and had a degree to show my intellectual abilities, I didn't even have a prospect as a possible mate. And though I wanted these things, the American dream, I had absolutely no clue how to begin to secure these. It was then that I realized I needed to make some changes in my life.

The next day, I went to see my therapist, Dr. Juan. This was going to be my last session with her so I wanted to make sure that I had gotten all that I could out of the sessions. I also wanted to make sure that I was not leaving with any baggage that I was supposed to drop off there during the last five years. I was finally going to tell her all that happened on that dreadful night.

As soon as I entered her office, I inhaled a wonderful smelling fragrance that reminded me of vanilla bean. Her office always brought a sense of calmness and security over me. Today was no different.

"Hello, Lisette," Dr. Juan said with a warm, welcoming tone. "How are you today?"

"I don't know exactly. I'm feeling a little strange. I feel like there is something inside of me that wants out, but I can't figure out how to get to it."

"Won't you sit down?" Dr. Juan gestured for me to sit while sitting down herself.

I told Dr. Juan how I was feeling, that I needed to make some changes in my life but wasn't sure where to start or how to go about it. I also told her that I was ready to tell her the rest of the story of the night I last saw James.

"The last thing you told me, Lisette, was that everything went dark. Now that you're ready, why don't you tell me the rest of the story?"

I closed my eyes and began to recall what happened that night. The vision was extremely vivid. I started to speak.

"After I came to, I could remember seeing blood on the walls in massive quantities. I couldn't move. I was frozen in place. I guess it was due to trauma and the unbearable pain. The next thing I heard were police sirens and the door being busted down. James and I were both rushed to the hospital. While we were at the hospital, I was charged with assault with a deadly weapon. I was told that I had stabbed James seventeen times and that he bled to death on the way to the hospital. However, with my multiple bruises (old and new), fractures and a lack of witnesses, the police could not determine whether it was self-defense or not. So even though I was charged with a felony, I was put on five years' probation instead of doing jail time. I was also required to see a therapist during my probation time. That's where you come in."

I opened my eyes. There! I had finally told Dr. Juan all that had happened from the beginning to the end. I felt myself exhale.

"Congratulations, Lisette!" Dr. Juan said as she gave me a warm nod and a slight grin. "I can see that you have finally come to terms with what happened that night and I am so glad for the progress that you have made. This is a giant step for you. As long as you continue on this path of healing and self awareness, you will find out how to make all of the necessary changes needed in your life."

"Thank you!" I said. "I know that you are right. Even though I'm not exactly sure how I'll go about everything, I know that it will work out in the long run. One immediate change that is definitely going to be a huge step in the right direction is that I have almost completed my probation. With this change, I can start applying for jobs in my field. Since the cleaning that I do at night is in the College of Social Work at the City University of New York, and my degree is in Social Work, I'll go there earlier than my scheduled work hours and try to network. I'll keep working at nights until I find another job and will take small steps towards making my life the one that I dream of."

"That's wonderful!" Dr. Juan proclaimed enthusiastically. She caught herself and calmed herself down before making her next statement. "Lisette, if you don't take anything else from our sessions, I want you to know that what happened between you and James was not your fault. Go ahead and live. If you were not meant to be alive, you would have died that night, but you didn't. You did what you had to do. Had I been in your situation, I might have done the same. I'd also like you to know that you are an incredibly strong woman. Don't ever forget that. Continue to make goals and seek to achieve them. You are worth it, and you deserve it."

After I thanked Dr. Juan, she wished me the best, and we said our goodbyes. After leaving her office, I went to see my probation officer to officially be cleared and off of papers. My probation was over.

During the following months, I diligently applied for positions in my field. I was still working as a maid but I was optimistic. Iris and I were becoming pretty good friends. I was beginning to feel closer to her than I had felt towards anyone in a long time. I even told her that I was considering finishing up my Master's degree. I only had a year left and could return to school once I had a day job. That way, I could work during the day and go to school at night. Iris agreed that my plan sounded like a good and plausible one. She also said she'd give me any support that I needed. It was then that I realized that I hadn't shared any of myself or my life with anyone other than my therapist for years. James was successful in isolating me from my family and friends. Even after he was gone out of my life, I was still living a life of isolation. I decided it was time to stop living in seclusion and to rekindle my relationship with my family. It was time to go home.

"Lissy!" I heard some voices calling my name and instantly knew who they were. No one called me Lissy outside of my family. It was my sister and brother. They were both calling my name in unison as I entered the front door of our family home. They greeted me with hugs and kisses. It felt like it had been forever since I had seen them.

"It's about time you made it home stranger!" my brother said. "We were beginning to think you'd forgotten all about us."

"It's so good to see you!" my sister said.

"It's good to see you all, too!" I said.

We all went into the kitchen and greeted our mother and father. It was Thanksgiving Day, and I was beginning to understand the real meaning of being thankful. I decided this holiday would be the day that I let my family know what had been going on in my life for the past several years. This would be another step toward the necessary changes in my life that would bring about some much needed healing.

My family gathered around the dinner table, and we bowed our heads as my father said grace. After he finished, we began to eat and talk about what was happening in our lives. I decided to speak last. I took a deep breath, held back the tears and told them all that had transpired since I last saw them. They listened intently. When I finished, there were several moments of silence. They were all sad and angry at the same time. I, on the other hand, was relieved and glad that I had waited until everything was over before I told them what happened.

My mother broke the silence and, in all her wisdom, calmly said, "Well, now baby, it's a good thing he's dead because if he weren't, I'd have to kill him."

This was the ice breaker that we all needed that caused everyone to laugh out loud. She then went on to say, "I'm proud of you for standing up for yourself, for being strong and for being courageous. I'm so sorry to hear what happened to you, but don't let your past hinder your present or your future. And don't you ever stay away from us or hide from us. We're your family. That's what we're here for."

Just as she finished her statement, an old familiar voice came through the door.

"Any food left for me?" Lionel asked jokingly as he walked into the dining room. Everyone laughed, and welcomed him in.

Lionel was a friend of the family. He had grown up with my brother and went to the military right out of high school. He kept in touch with everyone in the old neighborhood as often as possible, especially on holidays.

"Well, Lisette, fancy seeing you here. It's been how long? About ten years now? You ran off to college and didn't know anybody anymore," he said teasingly. "Good to see you," he said earnestly as he gave me a hug.

"It's good to see you too," I said.

We sat down and Lionel filled us all in on what had been going on in his life, the military, and his adventures in travel. We then filled him in on all that he had missed about us, including the story about James and me. After we were all done talking and eating, Lionel and I decided to take a walk and do some catching up.

"Lissy, I'm so sorry to hear about what happened to you. Why didn't you tell anyone? How could you keep that a secret from everyone? Don't you know how much your family cares about you? They would have intervened if you told them that James was abusing you."

I thought for a minute and replied, "Initially I thought it would stop. Then I accepted it and was too embarrassed to tell anyone. I thought it was somehow my fault. After the tragedy, I felt numb and confused. I didn't know what to think or who to trust anymore. I wasn't even sure who I was anymore. I just wanted it all to be a bad dream."

"Well, I'm glad that you walked away alive and that you are coming to terms with what happened. I'm also glad that you saw a therapist. That probably helped a lot."

"It did help. As a matter of fact, I can now say that I'm ready to live again. I'm ready to figure out what this life of mine is really meant to be. I am no longer afraid and ready to come out of hiding. I'm ready to leave the past behind me and start anew."

"Well, Ms. Lissy, I hope that I can be a part this new life of yours," Lionel said with a sheepishly gentle smile.

"Well, Lionel, I honestly don't know what the future may hold. But two things I do know for sure. I know that whatever the future may hold, I am ready for it. I also know not to rush things because all that we need to know, we will surely find out, in due time."

12. In Due Time, Erica Belcher, enbelcher@yahoo.com

13.

Accomplice

Sylvia Livingston

"He's gaining on us," Lisette yelled from the passenger seat.

Lisette felt the speed of the Chrysler 3000 surge faster as her sister, Janice, pressed down on the accelerator. Lisette glanced at the speedometer and saw that their speed was now registering one hundred miles per hour. The car suddenly jerked right, then left, causing Lisette to lose her balance. She stretched her hands out, catching the dashboard just in time to prevent herself from falling on her sister.

"Watch it, Lissy!" her sister yelled while downshifting. "Put your seatbelt on!"

"I got it . . . I got it," Lisette yelled back, righting herself. She snapped her seatbelt into place and saw the reason she became off balance was that they were rounding a curve.

"Where is he now, Lissy?" Janice asked while shifting gears again so they were back to their original speed.

Lisette glanced over her right shoulder and out the back window to see the Pontiac Grand Prix GT gaining. "He's on our tail and catching up fast."

With the arrival of another curve, Janice had to down shift again while the Pontiac Grand Prix surged ahead, barely slowing down to round the curve safely.

"Did you see that?" Lisette yelled. "He can't do that!"

"He just did," said Janice focusing on catching up. Janice shifted gears, pressed down on the accelerator and was able to regain her lead.

"We've got him now. There's only a mile left to go," Lisette observed.

In an instant, the Grand Prix was at Lisette's door. As if on cue, they were upon another curve. Janice down shifted to slow their momentum, but not before clipping the left front fender of the Grand Prix.

The last thing Lisette remembered was thinking, *Mom and Dad are going to kill us for wrecking their brand new car.*

"Can't these people learn how to pick up their stuff off the floor?"

Each time Lisette Donavan stepped inside a hotel room to clean, she never knew what she would find. Once she found a car in the bathtub—not a whole car, but pieces of a car, and grease everywhere. It was a good thing the occupants paid in cash and checked out before she entered their room because the bill would've cost them the price of three hotel rooms.

Deciding to start with the bathroom, Lisette made her way there, stepping over suit cases, clothes, and shoes. Upon reaching the bathroom, she found hand and bath towels strewn across the floor, not just in the customary place under the sink, but also by the commode, and in the bathtub.

Four years at the University of Alaska Anchorage, graduating magna cum laude in elementary education and receiving a teacher's certificate after a year of internship at a well-respected school in Anchorage, had not prepared her for being a hotel maid. The plan was after graduation, to return home to Kenai, Alaska, and teach at the local elementary school, a job promised to her after graduation from college. The contingency of spending a year in jail had not been part of the plan.

Lisette threw the gathered towels into her cart basket outside the hotel room and cringed when she heard a familiar voice call her name. She recognized it as being her co-worker and friend, Tonya, who seemed always in need of a favor.

Lisette pretended not to hear her until Tonya stood at the door of the room.

"Lissy, are you in here?"

Kneeling beside the commode, Lisette continued scrubbing as she answered Tonya. "I'm in the bathroom."

Tonya stepped inside the door jamb between the bedroom and the bathroom wearing the same maid's uniform as Lisette but snugger. With Tonya's curvaceous body and tan skin tones from her Latino heritage, men fell all over themselves trying to help her. This was a marked contrast to Lisette's pale skin tone and shapeless body that men ignored, especially when Tonya was around. Men paid for Tonya's purchases at coffee shops, grocery stores, and even hundred dollar purchases from clothing stores. But when Lisette was with Tonya, doors slammed in her face once Tonya walked through them.

Lisette looked up at her friend and asked the question she really didn't want to hear the answer to: "What can I do for you, Tonya?"

"I need a favor."

Lisette knew when Tonya asked for a favor it entailed either working overtime or on weekends. "What kind of favor?" Lisette asked.

"You know the guy I met in the lobby downstairs the other day?"

Lisette nodded affirmatively.

"Well, he wants to meet at Painters tonight at 5:30."

Lisette had heard of Painters. It was a new club in New York that required your name to be on an exclusive list. The only way your name gets on this is to be rich enough to pay your way on.

"It will take me at least 30 minutes to get home, change, and another 30 minutes for me to reach Painters."

There was always a long, drawn-out explanation on why she needed a favor.

"And?" Lisette coaxed.

Continuing to work, Lisette stood and began cleaning the shower.

"Could you clean my rooms? I promise I will make it up to you."

Tonya had made this promise on numerous occasions and never once had she reciprocated. Whenever Lisette needed a favor, Tonya was nowhere in sight. *All I have to do is say no*, Lisette thought, but she would lose one of the only friends she had in New York.

Tonya began tapping her long red polished nails on the door jamb, a habit that caused Lisette to cringe. It's like scraping fingernails across a chalk board.

"Okay . . . I will clean your rooms," Lisette gave in, not able to take the tapping any longer.

"Thank you so much!" Tonya exclaimed.

Tonya ran over to Lisette and gave her a hug. As she turned to leave she added, "I'll be leaving at four so you'll need to finish cleaning them by five o'clock."

"What?"

A glance at her watch told Lisette that she had less than two hours to complete both rooms.

"I overheard Mrs. Thomas tell Paula down on four yesterday that no one is to work overtime."

It's like Tonya to throw a twist into our agreement, Lisette thought. "Well, I suggest you leave now so I can finish my rooms and yours."

"Oh yeah, I almost forgot," Tonya said turning at the door. "There were two guys looking for you today, but Mrs. Thomas told them you had too much work to do to be disturbed." Tonya left the room without allowing Lisette to ask any questions.

Lisette didn't have time to contemplate who the two men were and why they were looking for her since she had so much work to do before five o'clock. She finished her and Tonya's rooms in time and when she reached her apartment, she could barely lift her legs onto her couch in order to rest them. The last thing she wanted was to hear someone knocking on her door.

"Li-sette!" called a male voice from the hallway.

Lisette immediately recognized the voice as being her nosy next door neighbor, Joshua.

The door was barely open before Joshua pushed his tall dark frame through it, sashayed across the floor, and flopped down on Lisette's couch.

"How can I help you, Joshua?"

Lisette closed the door and walked to the kitchen where she unhooked two tea cups from their holder and poured tea into them; she'd brewed earlier. She handed a cup to Joshua and sat down in the hard wooden chair opposite him.

"Girl," Joshua said with his long drawl. "You must be in some kind of trouble."

Joshua's effeminate manner and warm dark skin tones (from using the right face cream and foundation) gave a casual acquaintance a clue as to his chosen profession of being a drag queen performer.

"Two guys came looking for you today."

"There were two guys looking for me at work today as well," Lisette replied. "Did they say what they wanted?" Lisette couldn't imagine who they could be since she didn't know that many people in New York City, and the people she knew didn't know where she lived.

"I'm no genius, girl, but I would say they wanted you."

Joshua's habit of not getting to the point when telling a story was a constant annoyance for Lisette, especially today when she was too tired to follow his train of thought.

"Of course, they wanted me, but for what?" Lisette asked.

Joshua took a sip of tea before continuing. "I don't know. They were banging on your door like madmen. It was so loud they woke me up from my afternoon nap. And you know I need my afternoon nap, or I'll be a bear tonight at the club."

Lisette once again tried to steer Joshua back on track, asking, "What did they look like?"

"One was tall, in his 50's, the other in his 20's. They were both wearing black suits. You know, like the kind they wore in the movie *Men in Black*."

Whenever Joshua described someone he made reference to a character he'd seen in a movie. Many movies were ones Lisette had never heard of, but she'd heard of *Men in Black*.

I wonder if the men could have been my family, Lisette thought. Her father and brother could be in New York to visit her.

"What was their hair color?"

The possibility that they were in town without telling her sounded improbable, but she'd recently changed her cell number, and they wouldn't be able to reach her.

"I believe they both had red or auburn hair. I wasn't at my best since they woke me up from my beauty nap."

The color Joshua described didn't help her much since her father's hair was brown but had started to gray, so he sometimes colored it, and her brother's hair was chestnut brown.

Lisette stood, took the tea cup out of Joshua's hand, and ushered him out the door. "Don't worry, Joshua, everything will be okay," Lisette assured him.

"If you say so, but I tell you there was something shady about those guys."

Lisette could hear Joshua still mumbling about the two men after she closed the door. Reclaiming her seat on the couch, she picked up her cell phone and called her father but received no answer, so she called her brother Tommy, who picked up on the first ring.

"Is everything okay?" her brother asked.

The concern she heard in her younger brother's voice didn't surprise Lisette, since he had always seen himself as her protector. Even when they were growing up in Kenai, Tommy would take on the big brother role and fight older and bigger kids who upset her.

"Everything is fine," she assured him. "I called to find out if you and Dad are here in New York City."

"No . . ." Tommy answered. "Why do you ask?"

"Two guys came by my job and apartment today and with the description my neighbor gave me, I thought they might be you and Dad."

There was a long silence on the other end of the phone before Tommy said. "It wasn't us. Dad's in Anchorage, and I'm here in Kenai." There was another long silence. She could hear Tommy breathing and wondered why he was taking so long to continue. Finally, after what felt like hours he spoke. "Do you think they could've been from Anchorage?"

Lisette had to admit the thought of the two men being from Anchorage had crept into her consciousness but pushed the thought to the back of her mind. She'd hoped her troubles in Anchorage would forever be lost in the Juvenile records of Alaska.

"I'll be right there!" she heard her brother yell to someone on the other end of his phone. "Umm . . . Lissy, I gotta go. I'll call you later when I get free."

"Hey, have you heard from Janice?" Lisette asked before Tommy could hang up.

Lisette hadn't seen much of her sister since that ill-fated event.

"No, I haven't heard from her since she called home on Mom's birthday."

"Okay, tell Dad and Mom I love them."

"Will do."

Lisette hung up and began to feel a knot form in the pit of her stomach. *I really hope they're not from Alaska. It would be disastrous for my career if that terrible incident 10 years ago ruined my chances of getting a teaching job.*

Lisette's phone rang, jolting her back to the present. She hesitated before answering, afraid it was the men from Alaska. Finally after the fourth ring she answered.

"Hello?"

"Hey, Lisette, we need you to come in tonight," the male voice on the other end of the phone said. "LaQuita has called in sick again."

Lisette breathed a sigh of relief after recognizing the male voice as being her manager, Larry, at Zola's Coffee House and Muffins and not the two men she had now concluded as being from Alaska. Despite her tired feet, she agreed to work LaQuita's shift.

Larry took Lisette aside as soon as she walked through the back door.

"Hi, Larry," Lisette said. Staring at him with apprehension she couldn't help but think that maybe the two men had been there as well. Lisette held her breath waiting in anticipation for what he was about to say.

"There were two men asking about you this morning," he said.

Lisette's stomach jumped and a knot caught in her throat. She coughed to clear her throat before she trusted herself to talk. "Really. Did they say what they wanted?"

"They didn't say," Larry said. "They only handed me this card to give to you."

Lisette drew in a deep breath then took the business card from Larry's outstretched hand. Good or bad, she must know definitively who the men were. She turned the card over, and to her disbelief there was no identifying information written on it except for a crucifixion logo and a phone number with a New York City area code. At least it appeared they weren't from Alaska, but that didn't mean they weren't looking for her in New York as well. After much contemplation, Lisette decided to call the phone number and arranged a meeting for the next the day.

Nervously, Lisette walked through the restaurant's doors and immediately recognized the men by the black suits they were wearing. When she approached their booth, they both stood.

"Good afternoon, Ms. Donavan. We've been expecting you," said the man closest to her.

As Lisette slid in the booth across from them, she took in their appearance. She was surprised to find that one of the men was short and stout and the other was tall with a goatee and wearing a tunic, not at all how she pictured them in accordance with Joshua's description.

"I'm Pastor Harrison, and this is Mr. Hobbs."

"I think we should place our orders first before we discuss business, Pastor," interrupted Mr. Hobbs.

"You are quite right, Mr. Hobbs," Pastor Harrison agreed.

The pastor waved his hand toward a standing waitress to take their orders. Lisette opened her menu to find that the restaurant specialty was chicken and waffles. *An unusual combination*, she thought. After placing their orders, the pastor spoke first.

"Ms. Donavan, we are from the Divine Divinity School, and we would like to hire you as an elementary school teacher."

Lisette, who was taking a sip of water, started coughing uncontrollably. Mr. Hobbs reached across the table and began slapping her back until her coughing subsided. Lisette took one last sip of water to calm the tickle in her throat before she trusted herself to speak. "Did you say you want to hire me for a teaching job at your school?"

"Yes, we would," Mr. Hobbs said. We would like to hire you as an elementary school teacher at Divine Divinity. You see, Ms. Donavan, our school has a shortage of teachers."

"And we've received a generous donation allowing us to hire additional staff," Pastor Harrison finished.

"How did you get my name?" Lisette asked. "I've put in numerous applications all over the city, but I don't recall putting one in for your school."

"A mutual friend gave us your name but asked to remain anonymous," Pastor Harrison explained.

"Our school has a preschool and a K-12 school, but we really need an elementary school teacher and you come highly recommended," Mr. Hobbs said.

"Does it matter that I'm not that religious?"

"Not at all," Pastor Harrison answered. "We only ask that you don't discourage your students from seeking the word of God.

"Besides," Mr. Hobbs interjected. "We have a separate class for studying the Bible and Chapel once a week."

Everything they were saying appealed to Lisette, but she couldn't help thinking they were going to find out about her juvenile record.

"I hesitate to bring this up, but I feel I must tell you about an event that happened when I was a teenager."

Pastor Harrison reached for her hand and said. "You don't have to explain anything. Your anonymous reference told us everything."

Curious of whom her anonymous reference could be, Lisette decided that it was a question she could get answered later and extended her hand first to Pastor Harrison and then Mr. Hobbs and shook each, signifying her acceptance of their offer of a teaching job.

13. Accomplice, Sylvia Livingston,
      Sylvia.Livingston@yahoo.com

14.

I Want My Piece

Tremayne Moore

After getting off the Greyhound bus from Columbia, South Carolina, Lisette Donavan arrived around noon in New York City. She managed to get off the bus on 42nd Street, the sights and sounds of Time Square sending her mind reeling as she placed her hands on her hips. Whipping out her classic black power afro pick, she shaped her afro and checked her dark chocolate complexion to ensure any blemishes were covered with light blush. She had never been too fond of make-up—she knew she was beautiful. Even at five-four, 190 pounds, most of those in curves, Lisette knew how to attract men.

After putting her make-up away, she fixed her mind on the siblings she left behind. She was fed up with taking care of her sister, brother, mother, and father. Lissy was about to start her life over again.

No more drama from men. All men ever want to do is get next to me, from my mother's men to my own. I can't believe how she let those trifling men talk her into smoking crack and marijuana, turning our home into a crack fiend's playground. She was so busy getting high, she had no idea how many attacks I had to fend off. Although they touched me and I complained to her about it, I was considered the liar. Only my psychologist seemed to care, discovering my bipolar condition. At least these days seem more manageable with my anti-depressants.

Lisette's last relationship had been life-threatening. Openly proud about saving herself for marriage, her boyfriend had attempted to rape her; in self defense, she had sliced his well-cut body in multiple places. She was charged with aggravated assault, yet her boyfriend had only received a hand slap. Knowing that she couldn't live with the decision of the judicial system, a system corrupt at all levels, she got a Bachelor's Degree in Criminal Studies from South Carolina State University.

Lissy knew it was better to leave the area for something better. This charge would follow her, but she didn't have to stick around and be haunted and harassed.

God, I thank you that my being on medication saved me from going to jail. I believe if I had not been on medication, I would've served a year or two behind bars. Although I didn't serve any time for the charge, I learned a valuable lesson: that this is a man's world. How many times have I heard that?

Lissy continued to dwell on her childhood and her mother having multiple men over to the house. She remembered one of those men subjecting her to his clumsy, drunken groping. Thank God he had passed out before he could accomplish his mission. She never met her father, a Chicago inmate, and at this point in her life, she had little incentive to. She moved to South Carolina at the age of six. She was nineteen. Her childhood had literally been snatched out from under her. But she was in control now. She was ready to start her hair care business and live the American dream. Lisette would smile at the thought of being the CEO of Lissy Hair Company with an extravagant boardroom like the TV show, *The Apprentice.*

Lissy twirled herself around in Times Square, feeling right at home.

This is where people make it, here in New York City. If people like Donald can make it, I surely can. I know that's a blasphemous name for some people, his arrogance off-putting to some degree, but I can take his business ideas and make something for myself. Let me catch a cab to his Trump Tower on Fifth Avenue so I can see the American Dream that awaits me. If I can visualize it, I can believe it. He has brilliant ideas, and he took his dream to the next level. I am going to make something of myself. I refuse to be bound, begging, and fighting over two dollars and a biscuit. I want my piece of the American Pie, and I can have it even at the ripe age of twenty-eight. The only struggle I'll have to face is getting my feet on solid ground. If I can build enough capital, I can start my dream of being the power CEO of Lissy Hair Company with a customized hair care product line. Outside of my business, I can be an advocate against domestic abuse. I need to make a note to myself to take my medication when I get checked in. I know I don't have a lot of money, so I need to jot this down.

Lisette pulled out her voice recorder and started recording: "Once I get settled here in New York City, I need to start investing in things I love. This requires me to study small hair salons and beauty products. I need to hire a life coach and find mentors in the cosmetology field. I also need to learn about real estate and possibly take some cosmetology classes. This feels like a blueprint, and I'm so excited about this venture."

Lissy decided to take a walk (more like a power walk) back to the Waldorf-Astoria and informed the manager that she had arrived in New York today.

"You got a criminal past?"

"No! I didn't kill anybody, and I believe in doing the right thing," Lissy gave him a look of wide-eyed innocence.

"We do random criminal checks on our employees. Our motto is integrity and ethics. Anyway, here's your uniform and report to work at 7:30 A.M. tomorrow. You stepped in at the right time. We'll need you to fill out your paperwork before starting."

Lissy almost frowned at the uniform, but she smiled because the manager was staring at her like she was a piece of rotisserie gold chicken!

Lissy groaned at the hideous uniform.

This is so not my style. It needs so much tailoring for a body like mine, she sighed. *Here I am a maid. I was making good money in South Carolina as a legal analyst and now I have to settle for this. My family was counting on me to protect the image, provide for them, and now I feel like I'm poverty-stricken! I still want my piece of the American Pie, and I'm going to get it! I refuse to let my criminal background in South Carolina get the best of me; hopefully I will still be able to maintain my job in this economy. I know it's hard to get a job if you're unemployed. Chances are better if you are employed. I declare that I am the CEO of Lissy Hair Company, and I'm a force to be reckoned with!*

Preparing to embrace the humiliation of being hired help, Lissy caught the bus to the hotel. She made it right on time to be greeted by another maid.

"Good morning, Lisette. My name is Mary. You'll be working with me today."

"Good morning, Mary. You can call me Lissy."

Mary was the same height as Lisette, five-four, and weighed about 190 pounds, too. Mary, however, had golden hair with streaks of red in it. There wasn't much time for idle chat as she was being trained while observing Mary. The course of the day seemed to fly, with names, and faces, and people she was expected to learn as regular and exclusive clients. *So much to remember and so many opportunities to get it wrong*, she sighed to herself. Mary warned her no matter how much the clients said or revealed, she was not to engage them. She was the help. That was it.

"Some are very open about their situations—some are about to get married, some are there for travel, and then there are some who are just there for one-night stands," Mary informed her.

Lisette thought to herself, *If my man was caught here for a one-night stand, I would definitely be behind bars because I'd murder them both!*

The ladies decided to walk across the street for a hamburger at lunchtime. Mary noticed how withdrawn Lisette had become since their earlier shift.

"How's your family?" Mary asked.

"Fine," she uttered quickly. Lisette tried to keep her words few.

"How old are you?"

"Twenty-eight."

"Where are you from?"

"South Carolina."

"You have a boyfriend?"

"No."

"Are you a lesbian?"

"*What?*"

"Do you *date?*"

"No."

"How was your last relationship?"

"I'd rather not say."

"Oh, you can tell me, girl."

"We only met this morning. No offense, but I don't trust you." Lissy glared.

"I knew there was some angle with you."

"Why are you judging me so fast when you don't *know* me?" Lissy snapped.

"Well, I don't trust you, Lissy. You come out of nowhere and get hired just like that? Seems suspicious." Mary narrowed her eyes.

"Let's get back to work." Lissy gathered her trashed and headed back.

From that point forward, Mary continued to drill Lisette to see if she would snap. But Lissy wasn't dumb. She took her medication and prayed that she wouldn't slip into her past. As Mary prodded, Lissy remained silent as if she knew anything she said would be held against her. But there was one question that Lissy *would* answer.

"What was your degree in?"

"Criminal Studies," Lissy stated casually.

"Oh, so you're one of those *educated* women, huh?"

"You could say that."

"Now, don't judge me, Lissy, because *I* don't have a college education."

"I'm not here to judge you. I'm here to get my piece of the American Pie, and you can too, with or without education. You have talents and goals. I hope this isn't the sum total of your life." Lissy pounded the pillow of the hotel bed they were cleaning.

Mary stopped in her tracks, looking at Lissy with respect. "You're the first person to say that to me. I see so many people fighting for their jobs, and you're the first person to tell me that I am so much more than this. I always thought that I would be secure in this, and I would have to put on a false face that I'm happy. I was so determined to not let you take my job, but now I see that you don't want to take over my job," she smiled. "You want to take over the world," she chuckled.

"Now you understand me, Mary. I needed to get away from where I was in order to become somebody, and I believe I found my place in this city. Are you with me?"

"I am. You know, you're not so bad after all, Lissy."

"Thank you." Lissy managed a small smile.

As the day drew to a close, Lissy went to the bus stop to head back to her home. Lissy got on the bus and started praying. "Thank you, Lord, for getting me through my first days at work. I am so glad you turned things around for me. If I didn't learn anything from today, I learned that you have to give people a chance no matter how much they want to get into your personal space. Some people will only care about themselves because they're living in fear, or want the accolades for themselves, and some people really *do* have the heart to care. I guess this is all about separating the wheat from the tares. I pray that Mary will find out what talent You gave her so she doesn't have to work as a maid for the rest of her life. I have determined not to let that happen to me. Until my business takes off, I need this steady income. I know I have fought some demons in my past, and I may face some in the future. But I am determined to fight until someone's life is impacted by my talent for the glory of Your name," she finished.

As she prepared to sleep that night, Lissy turned to Proverbs where it says, "Without a vision, the people perish."

I have my vision and I want my piece of the American Pie. But more importantly, I am thankful that I have my place in God's Kingdom. She closed her eyes with the expectation that tomorrow would bring her even closer to that dream.

14. I Want My Piece, Tremayne Moore,
tremayne_moore@yahoo.com

15.

Maid to Survive

Karen Randolph

"On Count I of Assault and Battery, we, the jury, find the Defendant, Lisette Donavan, guilty. Sentencing will be scheduled. Until then, you will remain in the custody of the Palm Beach County Sheriff's Office. Court is adjourned," the judge said, banging the gavel on the wooden plank. That was twelve short years ago, Lisette was sixteen-years old. She had been arrested after going over to the house of some girl for a random fight. She could barely remember why. Perhaps the girl had slept with Lisette's boyfriend; perhaps the girl threatened her. Try as she might, she could not remember, the details escaped her. So many things had happened since that time. Finally, Lisette was on the right path, or so it seemed.

"Wow, I am finally here!" Lisette thought to herself as she looked around her small one bedroom, one bathroom, New York City apartment. It wasn't much, but it was clean and all she could afford. She would have rather been moving into a Penthouse apartment at Trump Towers, but starting over is hard to do, especially when you are working as a maid. Lisette was most grateful of the fact that she wouldn't have to sleep on her best friend's lumpy sofa bed another night. She was also grateful that Tawanda quickly came to her rescue three years ago. Before then, Lisette never would have thought she would have even ended up in the city that never sleeps. She was a modest girl from humble beginnings. The Big Apple's skyline would never be seen from any window of her twelfth floor apartment. She looked out the

window and was faced with a weathered red brick wall. When she looked down, there was nothing there but garbage dumpsters and trash on the ground in the dark alley.

At twenty-eight years old, Lisette held a bachelor's degree in business administration and had no children. She had done everything right, including falling in love and marrying the man of her dreams.

"Well, I better get out of these clothes," Lisette mumbled, which were dampened with sweat from moving boxes and heavy furniture with Tawanda's help. "Tomorrow is going to be busy so I better get my rest," she said aloud with a sigh as she turned on the water to the shower. Steam had filled the small bathroom by the time she removed her clothes. She stepped in the shower and the hot water felt great on her skin. It melted away the pain of moving the boxes and furniture earlier today. Thirty minutes had passed when the shockingly cold water hit her skin and snapped her out of her trance-like thoughts. She quickly turned off the water and reached for her towel, which she wrapped around her pleasantly plump but curvy brown-skinned, five-four body. As she sat on her new twin-size bed, looking in her overnight bag for her lotion, she began to think about how she had arrived at this point in her life.

She must have drifted off as soon as she finished putting on the lotion. Before she knew it, the alarm clock was blaring, alerting Lisette that it was time to rise and grind! Today was Thanksgiving and she knew Mr. Gibson would want everything to be perfect for the arrival of his family. Lisette was a maid for billionaire real estate tycoon, Ty Gibson, and his wife, Nadine. To the Gibsons, she was Emily Richardson. Nadine was a trophy wife. Her one and only job was to look good at all times, especially while on the arm of her tall, dark, and handsome husband when attending philanthropic fundraisers all over the country. Nadine made sure "Emily" knew that it was her job to keep the twelve-room mansion picture perfect at all times. Nadine ensured this by leaving a long detailed list of things to do every single day. Lisette didn't understand why they needed such a huge mansion when it was only the two of them. Nadine certainly didn't look like she intended to give her husband any of the children he wanted anytime soon. Lisette knew Nadine didn't want to give up that brick house figure to have any babies because that meant the possibility of those wide hips spreading even wider. Plus, Nadine was secretly taking birth control pills.

Lisette would have to make her rounds first thing to make sure all the amenities were taken care of to the specifications of the incoming family members which, of course, were on her to-do list. Lisette would have to make sure all of the linens were fresh, the thirteen bathrooms were sparkling, and the oversized white towels were fluffy and rolled perfectly on the cart next to the indoor heated pool. While wiping down the bathroom counter, Lisette thought about her family back in South Florida. Her momma was probably running around the kitchen like a chicken with her head cut off trying to make everything perfect for the arrival of her siblings. Lisette was the middle child of three. She knew exactly what her momma was cooking up—all the traditional fixings for her children and husband. Being away from home reminded Lisette about the time she was away in jail. While the Donavans weren't rich, they were what America considered middle class. Cordelia was a stay-at-home mom and Pierre was an attorney. Nevertheless, the Donavans still were able to give their kids most of what they had ever wanted. After getting out of jail, Lisette promised her parents that she would stay out of trouble and kept her word by working at her father's firm as a paralegal. Lisette also had a side job making and selling jewelry. Her company's name was Beadiful Creations.

Everything was going fine in her life until she met DeVaughn Williams. He worked for the local parcel service and he persistently tried to get her attention each time he came into the office. He flirted with her daily, and in time, she began to flirt with him. When DeVaughn finally got up the nerve to ask her out, she declined. One night soon thereafter, Lisette ended up running into DeVaughn at her neighborhood's coffee shop. She was surprised to see DeVaughn in her neighborhood because she was certain he didn't live in the area. Lisette remembered that day like it was yesterday.

"Hey beautiful lady, can I have this seat?" DeVaughn whispered into her right ear. When she turned around, DeVaughn was standing behind her looking more handsome than she had remembered him being. The manly smell of his cologne engulfed her nose. At first, she hesitated, then replied with a flirtatious, "Sure." He sat down and they fell into a comfortable conversation pattern. It was like they had known each other forever. Before they knew it, hours had passed by. Soon after seeing DeVaughn at the coffee shop, Lisette accepted DeVaughn's invitation to dinner once, twice, and before long, they were in a relationship.

The relationship was going great, and she began to see qualities in DeVaughn that were exactly what she had wanted in a man. He was five-nine, dark-skinned, very handsome, and hard working. He was very attentive to her every want and need. Within twelve months, they married and moved to the suburbs of West Palm Beach, Florida. For a change, life was good, and Lisette was enjoying every minute of it.

They had been married for one and a half years and preparing to celebrate their anniversary when all hell broke loose. The honeymoon was clearly over. All of a sudden, DeVaughn became overly possessive. He wanted to know who she was talking to and for what. She had a list of things memorized of what she could and could not do. One day, while she was cleaning, she came across a file stuffed with her personal information and red flags flew up. She had never seen the file folder before and wondered where it had come from. She held the folder open with shaky hands and took a deep breath. There were copies of her cell phone bill with numbers highlighted in neon yellow, pictures of her at work, at the coffee shop, at the mall, and various other places she frequented. Once she went through the entire file, she knew instantly that the day at the coffee shop didn't happen by chance. DeVaughn was stalking her. No wonder it felt like they knew each other when they first met because he knew her every move. Now it all made sense. That's how he knew what perfume she liked to wear, how he knew she would love the Cheesecake Factory when he suggested it for their first date.

Their relationship was crumbling before her eyes and Lisette was pissed! She immediately went to call her parents, but had second thoughts because she figured if he was monitoring her cell phone records, then he may have had the phone line tapped as well. She could not risk him knowing she knew all about his lies. Lisette began to plot about how she was going to get out of this situation because she knew DeVaughn was not going to let her go without a fight. She decided to put the file in a manila envelope under the floor mat of her car because he would never think to look there. Then, she slowly began to pack up her belongings and ship them to her best friend. Of course, she had already filled Tawanda in on what was happening and "the plan." DeVaughn would ask periodically why the closet was looking so thin, and she would tell him that she was doing spring cleaning and donating some of her old stuff to charity.

One Friday night, she came home to find him scurrying about. He was obviously looking for something because drawers were pulled out and papers were all over the place. She asked him if she could help him find whatever it was he was looking for. He replied with an angry "No!" She knew exactly what he was looking for—the folder!

At dinner, it seemed as though he had calmed down, but she still had her guard up. DeVaughn was like a ticking bomb. He could explode at any minute. After cleaning the kitchen, she was exhausted. She was lying in bed in the dark when DeVaughn exited the shower. She could see that he was naked. She did not want to go there with him, so she pretended to be asleep. Lately, this was the signal that sexual relations would soon follow. She was surprised when he laid flat on his back without touching her. DeVaughn must have been waiting on her to go to sleep when he pounced on her. She must have been sleeping hard because when she woke up she was on her back, naked, and he was on top of her, holding her wrists down to the bed. He had a wild look in his eyes as he demanded that she open her legs. When she refused, he slapped her so hard she could taste blood in her mouth. He growled at her, "I know you have that file, but it doesn't matter now because you belong to me." DeVaughn demanded again that she open her legs because he wanted what belonged to him. Again, she denied him, and he hit her again, but this time with his fist, knocking her unconscious.

When Lisette came to, she could see she was no longer in the bed but in the basement and tied to a chair. Her body was so sore, it was throbbing. She clicked into survival mode. She held her breath so she could hear any movement upstairs. She didn't. *DeVaughn must be gone.* So she looked around frantically for something to cut the rope with. She found a small dull kitchen knife and started working on cutting the rope from her hands. When she finally made it upstairs, she didn't take a chance trying to gather more of her things; she just headed for her spare keys and purse. She stopped at a payphone and called Tawanda to let her know the plan was in action. She drove to a motel to get cleaned up before boarding the train to New York City. She knew that DeVaughn would have people looking for her, so she changed her entire identity. She had her long black locks cut into an updated sassy style and colored it a brownish-red. She also lost some weight and changed her name to Emily Richardson. She became a maid because homeowners paid under the table, so there was no need for a social security number.

"Momma, I'm so glad you made it safely." Mr. Gibson's booming voice brought Lisette back to reality. Ugh, Mr. Gibson's family was arriving one by one. First, his momma and her little toy Yorkie.

"I can't stand dogs," Lisette said under her breath. But Mrs. Gibson-Ashton didn't hear her because she was too busy telling Ty about his cousin coming from Florida to visit with them this year. Lisette pulled the list out of her apron and checked it again; she only had five guests coming, Mr. Gibson's mother, his brother, his two sisters, and his aunt. Now she had to get another room ready for yet another guest. As if on cue, the door bell chimed. Since she was upstairs preparing the room, Mr. Gibson answered the door, and she heard them conversing downstairs. She stopped dead in her tracks when she heard his voice; the deep velvety voice of the newly arrived cousin was DeVaughn. No freaking way!

"Oh my God, oh my God, how am I going to get out of this house?" Lisette was now sweating profusely. She could barely breathe and began having a panic attack. Out of all the families in the world, how the hell did she end up working for DeVaughn's cousin? "I've got to get out of here," Lisette said to herself.

Lisette quickly decided to call Nadine upstairs and tell her she needed to leave for the day because her cycle was starting, she was cramping badly, and she didn't have any sanitary napkins. She was sure Nadine would understand, woman to woman, what she was going through. The lie worked, and Lisette flew out the door and down the street to the train. She immediately called Tawanda on her cell phone. "You ain't gonna believe who showed up on the Gibson's doorstep today," Lisette screamed into the phone at Tawanda. "What am I going to do?"

"Well, we are going to have come up with a plan, Lissy. I'll meet you at your house in ten minutes," Tawanda replied. Once at home, Lisette could not stop pacing. Back and forth, back and forth across the tiny living room floor she paced trying to figure out how in the world she didn't know DeVaughn was Mr. Gibson's cousin. She had looked through all of Mr. Gibson's photo albums and didn't remember seeing the face of DeVaughn, not once. The keyhole made a noise and she knew it was Tawanda because, besides the super, she was the only other person with a key.

"Okay, what ideas do you have because you know you cannot go back there and work tomorrow. DeVaughn will surely figure out that your name isn't Emily," Tawanda said with confidence.

"I don't know. What do you think I should do?" Lisette asked.

"I think there are only two options you have, my dear friend," Tawanda said confidently.

"I can't keep running forever, but I know he will recognize me as soon as he lays his eyes on me. Oh, Tawanda, how did I end up in this mess?" Lisette cried out, tears of frustration falling from her face, forcing her eyes to turn bloodshot red. In her heart, she knew DeVaughn would never stop searching God's green earth for her. Like he said, she belonged to him. There was only one thing she could think to do.

It was four in the morning when they arrived at the Gibson's house, dressed in all black, their hair covered with black ski caps. They waited until all the lights were out in the house before they exited Tawanda's car. Since Lisette had a key to the house and knew where all the security cameras were, they snuck into the mansion like professionals. They climbed the stairs to the bedroom she had cleaned earlier for DeVaughn. He was in the shower, so they positioned themselves in the room to wait until he fell asleep before they made their move. As soon as DeVaughn was snoring heavily, Tawanda quickly tied his wrists and feet to the bed. When the ropes were secure Lisette climbed into position. She mounted DeVaughn and whispered in his ear, "Hey, baby, I've missed you but you tried to kill me so I am going to have to kill you!"

As soon as DeVaughn realized he wasn't dreaming, she put the pillow over his face, smothering him to death as he struggled to get free. After about five minutes of holding the pillow firmly over his face, he stopped moving. As she was untying DeVaughn, so the death could look natural, she turned to see Mr. Gibson standing in the doorway and froze. They didn't even hear anyone come into the room.

"Emily, what are you doing?" Mr. Gibson called out to her in almost a whisper.

15. Maid to Survive, Karen Randolph, Randolphkd@aol.com

16.

Lissy Transforming

Angelia Vernon Menchan

Lisette Donavan walked from her probation officer's office with a copy of her brand spanking new bachelor's degree in her hands. Lissy looked at it several times in disbelief. There was nothing in her life that had prepared her to be a college graduate—not her drug-addicted mother who introduced her to turning tricks at fourteen, and it certainly wasn't the man she had almost killed for trying to introduce her sister to the same mess. That night from eight years ago flashed in her head, causing her to shiver. She could see it as clearly as the blue sky above her dreadlocked head.

"Mr. Jack, I'm not doing that. My sister, Lissy, said I could be anything I want to be. She promised me she would be the last one of us to ever have to have sex with men for money. Mama died two years ago from HIV, and it's a miracle Lissy never got anything. She's working hard at the hotel taking care of Jon and me. Please leave me alone."

Fourteen-year old Janay pleaded with the landlord of the dilapidated house she lived in with her older sister and brother. Jon was sixteen and working nights at a factory while Lissy cleaned rooms at the Red Roof Inn. Janay was just as lovely as her sister, with skin the color of mahogany that glowed with health and locks that hung past her shoulders. The siblings had a tough life, but they had stayed together, and Lissy made sure they were fed and healthy. Their mother had died when Lissy was barely eighteen, but she had taken care of them. She had stopped working the streets and worked hard to present a good image for them to model.

"Girl, I don't care what you say. Your sister is late on the rent, and if she won't give me what I want, I will get it from you."

Janay screamed as the tall, heavy man advanced towards her, squeezing her eyes shut. Before he could touch her, Janay heard a choking sound. Slowly opening her eyes, she saw Mr. Jack lying on the floor with blood pouring from his head. Lissy stood over him with a broken baseball bat in her hands.

The memory of that night lingered in Lissy's mind like bitter ash. Two days later, she had been arrested and taken to jail and Jon and Janay were left to fend for themselves, living with their holier-than-thou Aunt Geneva. Lissy spent four years in jail before Mr. Jack was arrested for child molestation, and which led to her being granted a new trial and then released. Although she was released, she still had an attempted murder charge on her record. She also had no idea where Jon was. Janay had done okay. She was now twenty-four and the mother of two children. She had graduated from high school, and, with Lissy's help, she was working as a nurse's assistant and taking classes at night to become a nurse. The two of them lived with the children in a nice three-bedroom apartment downtown.

There were two things that drove Lissy; they were finding Jon and overcoming her past to get a job in the field in which she had educationally excelled. She had just received a degree in finance, but she knew with her record, she had a long way to go to get there, but she was determined. She had overcome worse.

Walking into the Hilton for her shift as a maid, Lissy could only smile. Before going to prison, she had worked in a low-end hotel. Now she was at the Hilton, of all places, but the fact remained, she was a criminal in the eyes of the world and those in the know felt she should be pleased with where she was with her lot in life. Her supervisor had told Lissy to her face that she should be glad she could clean up after the wealthy and receive $15.00 per hour for it with her background. Lissy had learned to suck down the retorts that sprang to her mouth because she wanted nothing to stand in the way of what she wished to accomplish. She would continue to clean the rooms and mind her business. But her sights were set on the future because, in addition to finding Jon and getting a great job, she wanted to know what it was like to be loved, truly loved, the way a man loved a woman, who loved him back.

Janay looked out the window and was glad to see her sister's serious face. Lissy was a beautiful woman, but her face was always shrouded in seriousness. Pulling open the door, Janay embraced her sister, kissing her all over her face. She knew there was something that would make her smile. The girls heard their auntie and ran into the room, jumping into the fray. For several minutes, the Donovan girls were happy.

"What is that I smell?" Lissy asked, sniffing the air.

"Pork chops and cabbage. I figured you would be hungry after working your shift and seeing your P.O."

Smiling, Lissy pulled the scarf from her head, allowing her waist length locks to unravel sensuously. Immediately, she looked like a different person, even in her maid's uniform, Janay looked at her big sister, smiling.

"Come on, Lissy, come eat with me, and tell me about your day. The girls have eaten already."

Sitting across from one another, the two women talked about day-to-day things until finally, Lissy pulled her degree from her pocket and placed it on the table. Janay picked it up and immediately started praise dancing around the kitchen, but stopped short when she saw the tears coursing down her sister's ebony cheeks. Racing over, she wrapped her arms around her older sister, allowing her to cry. It was very unusual to see tears in Lissy's eyes. After several minutes, Lissy pulled away, walking to look down from the third floor window.

"J., it doesn't mean anything. For four years, I have been cleaning toilets and changing nasty sheets to put food in my mouth and pay for a place to lay my head and so many doors have been shut in my face. I know for a cold, hard fact that no one will hire me. Once they see the arrest record for attempted murder, I will be just another hood chick." Bitterness laced the words, causing

Janay to feel guilty because she knew if it hadn't been for defending her, Lissy wouldn't be in this predicament.

"Lissy, I am sorry. I wish you hadn't defended me."

Turning sharply, Lissy held a finger to her lips. "J., I would do it all again for you. Please, don't feel guilty. What I need is for Mr. Jack to tell the truth. His being arrested helped get me a new trial, but he maintains that I hit him because I was jealous of you. He told people he had once been my John, and that in my jealousy I hit him. He was once that, I didn't lie, so here I am. We all pay for our transgressions. And as mama's holy-roller sister so eloquently says, "I'm doing good for a former ho, daughter of a crack addict, who never knew her daddy. I should be grateful."

"Girl, Aunt Geneva is just jealous. It makes her mad that you got out and did something with yourself. She only let me live there because she got money for me. She always talking about God, but there ain't a godly bone in her evil body."

Turning to look at her sister, Lissy smiled slightly. "J., do you believe in God."

"Yes, ma'am, from the top of my head to the bottom of my feet. Only God could have brought me and you through all we have been through and landed us here. We have a nice apartment, two great kids, each other. Though we aren't thrilled with our jobs, we have jobs. Lissy, you know only God could have done all that."

"Then who put us in that situation? Did God do that, too?"

"No, ma'am, mama did. She had freewill and her will was to do drugs. She grew up in a nice home, she wanted to chase thrills, and that's what she did. We can't blame God for Mama's mess, and God took us through all that so that when you are running your own business, and I am running a clinic, we will appreciate all we have."

"How did you get so smart, so young?"

"Living . . ."

Lissy pulled her little sister in her arms, wishing she had all that confidence and faith. The vibrating phone in her pocket made her pull away. She was surprised to see her P.O.'s number. After this morning, she was done with probation and college.

"Lissy, this is Anna DeVore. I have an appointment scheduled for you with an attorney tomorrow morning. He might be able to help you locate your brother and get your record expunged."

Hope jumped in Lissy's throat, but she swallowed it quickly. She had learned to expect the worse.

The next morning, Janay was stunned when her sister walked in the room. Her locks were pulled back from her face, her skin was glowing, and she had on a rich red lip gloss. She was also wearing a dark red dress and three-inch heels. She had never seen her sister look more beautiful. Lissy usually lived in jeans, scarves, and loafers.

"Well, excuse me, Diva. Who are you?"

"Is it too much? I have a meeting with an attorney this morning who may help with my record and may potentially help me find Jon."

Closing her eyes for several minutes, Janay prayed. "Lissy, let Jon go and focus on you."

Lissy didn't like the way Janay's voice sounded,

"Why . . . What do you know?"

Again, Janay's eyes closed. When she opened them, she knew she would have to tell her sister the truth.

"Sit down . . ."

Doing as her sister asked, a sense of dread entered Lissy's belly.

"Lissy, Jon isn't lost. He simply doesn't want to be found,"

"What are you talking about?"

"When you left, he became really wild, and hung out with the wrong crowd. Aunt Geneva put him out, sent him away, as I told you. What I didn't tell you is that about six months ago, I was in the city, and I saw this beautiful girl dancing and immediately I knew it was our brother. Lissy, he had a transforming operation and is dancing under the name JonDona."

Nausea pooled in Lissy's throat.

"As a stripper?"

"No, actually not, as an actual Off-Broadway dancer, and JonDona wants nothing to do with us, Aunt Geneva, and the life he left behind. He's quite happy being someone else. The only reason he talked to me is because he wanted to make himself clear. No one knows that he was ever a man, and he would like it to stay that way."

"Why didn't you tell me?"

"Lissy, you have too much going on, and I knew that you would never find Jon Anthony Donavan, no matter how hard you tried. It was God who brought me to that place that day. But this morning when I saw you all dressed up, I knew you needed to know, so you could focus on you. Lissy, you have done all you could for mama, me, and Jon It is now time to do you. No more excuses. Because the truth is, your background isn't holding you back as much as you are holding yourself back."

Janay's words rained down around Lissy's shoulders like warm spring water, and she knew her baby sister was right about it. Leaning over, she kissed her forehead before walking out the door.

Oh my, what a Goddess. That cannot be the Lisette Donavan.

Richard Blayburn literally squirmed in his seat as he watched Lissy walk across the room towards him. She looked a bit vulnerable and very nervous, but she was lovely. He had read her file and knew everything there was to know about her life and past, but he was totally unprepared for the way his heart raced in his chest. He was smitten. Standing up, he waved to her. Stumbling, she had to still herself because Ms. DeVore had failed to tell Lissy that her attorney would make Morris Chestnut look ugly. Her stomach did flips as she reached to offer her hand. At that moment, she realized she hadn't been touched intimately in years. For several minutes, they stood, shaking hands, until finally she pulled hers away. Clearing his throat, he introduced himself.

"Hello, Ms. Donavan. I am Richard Blayburn, and I'm here to take over your life . . ."

"My life . . ." Embarrassment flooded his milk chocolate face, causing him to smile slightly, showing his slightly crooked but dazzling teeth.

"I mean your case. Please have a seat."

For two hours, they went through the case. She left nothing out, telling him all the dirty details. He listened, never jotting down a word in his notebook. His eyes were fastened on hers the whole time.

"So, Mr. Blayburn. Do you think you can help me?"

"Umm, my name is Richard and absolutely. This is a simple matter, actually. Hasn't anyone told you that before?"

"No, I hadn't asked anyone. I wanted to get my degree, save up enough money for an attorney, and then do this. By the way, how much will this cost me?" Her heart raced in her throat because she was afraid she might not have enough money and because she had a strong desire to bite him.

"Umm, it won't cost much. I will have my partner handle it. He should be able to get Jack to sign something in a day or two and the expunged records will be a mere formality."

"Your partner . . ."

"Yes, ma'am, because I don't date my clients, and Ms. Donovan, you and I will be dating. And on our first date, I will tell you how former bad-boy Richard Blayburn became an attorney."

Sliding his card across to her, he winked, walking from the restaurant. Looking upwards, Lissy said, "Okay, God, I am finally listening."

16. Lissy Transforming, Angelia Vernon Menchan,
     acvermen@yahoo.com

17.

Lisette Donavan's American Dream

Cheryl B. Williams

"Lissy!" Ms. Hattie shouted, while thumping Lisette on the back of the head. "Girl, did you forget that you're sitting in the basement of the Rich Master's Hotel," Ms. Hattie teased. "He just lets you have a little break every now and then. Remember, we's just the hired help." Hattie laughed and said, "Really, Lissy—I think you forget that I put my twenty years of service to this hotel on the line to get you hired—and with your record, it wasn't easy. Sometimes you seem so ungrateful. You sitting there like you'd rather be at that college than at work. If you ask me, in a way, it's that college that got you into the mess that gave you a record. Your people still can't seem to get it together 'cause of you—your Mom and Pop can't sleep at night worrying 'bout you. Your little sister, Cindi, scared to go away to college, and the chile has a scholarship! Your parents had to even make your brother, Andy, come home from that college to keep him from doing something crazy. Andy still wants to get that guy for hurting his big sister.

All the while Lisette was thinking . . . *there she goes again, throwing up my past, telling me how I've hurt my family and how I'm ungrateful for this hotel maid job in New York . . . big deal. It's still a hotel maid job, and hey, I'm a college graduate, even if I didn't complete the fifth year. I did earn my B.S. But most of all, she still has to bring up the fact that I trusted a man enough to allow him into my heart. I know Ms. Hattie doesn't mean any harm. She's a smart lady and wise, too. My great-aunt Rosa told me to do whatever Hattie says to do 'cause she wouldn't steer me wrong. I love my Auntie, and I've grown to love her best friend,*

Hattie, who has been like a sister to Auntie since they were little girls.

"Lissy!" Ms Hattie shouted, interrupting Lisette's pleasant thoughts. "You doing it again! I've been talking for five minutes and you acting like I'm not even in the room! What's wrong! I said you just need to be more grateful!"

Lisette replied, "Nothing is wrong, Ms. Hattie. I'm just thinking!" But Lisette knew she couldn't fool old Hattie. Lisette mumbled under her breath, "I'll just say what she really wants to hear." She thought to herself, *you would think that she had actually gotten my record expunged and found me a job with a Fortune 500 Company the way she talks on and on sometimes about being grateful.*

So Lisette said out loud, "Ms. Hattie, you know I'm so grateful for you." Under her breath Lisette said in unison with Hattie: "Well act like it!"

Hattie continued saying, "'Cause when I came in this break room, you were more than a million miles away—you were in a different galaxy. You had the strangest look on your face. Your eyes were glazed and you had your arms wrapped tightly around yourself. What's wrong with you girl?"

Of course I said, "Nothing!" But Hattie was too perceptive to accept that response and just gave me a strange look. "Lissy, listen here girl, you done come too far. You getting stronger each day. Old Hattie can feel that you learning how to forgive yourself and most important, you learning how to trust again. Don't backtrack baby. The look I saw on your face worries me 'cause it was that same sad look on you when you first came to your Auntie Rosa on that cold February afternoon." *Hattie remembered a scrawny, blank-staring young lady that walked into her friend's apartment. Hattie knew all about the young lady's horrific background and how her parents sent her to her great aunt in New York to get away from her painful environment. Hattie had promised her friend that she would help her great-niece get a job and would be a friend to the reclusive, lost-looking young woman.*

Lisette thought to herself: *Hattie was right . . . I am getting stronger . . . becoming the Lisette that everyone once knew. I'm beginning to look and feel like the athlete I once was from the daily running . . . it's clearing out my mind, too. But every now and then, the cold reminder of the devastation I experienced would creep up my spine like prickly needles, and my mind would go back to what led me to New York.* There were days when it was as though Lisette was experiencing an outer body phenomenon that she had no control of and she would re-live the pain that led to her felony record like déjà vu. . .

It was a crisp fall afternoon nearly five years ago, and Lisette was overjoyed to be among the National Merit Scholars being honored at the welcoming brunch. Her parents were so proud of her and so were her younger sister and brother, Cindi and Andy. Her Dad said, "Andy, next year will be your turn, then your baby sister's. I'm proud of you kids." Lisette's Dad beamed with pride while her mother's eyes became glassy.

Lisette missed her family but she was enjoying college life and was doing well in her classes. She thought to herself: *My five-year Business Management/MBA Program is challenging, but I like a challenge.* However, little did she know that she would face a challenge that would change her life forever. Lisette noticed this fine upper classman, Alex Cooper, who seemed to constantly watch her. He finally approached her and did so on several occasions and each time Lisette expressed no interest and said no to his request for a date. Lisette thought to herself: *I'm on a mission. I am nobody's 'fresh meat.' I have no time for, nor want any part of this college love thing.*

At graduation, Lisette and her girls were so happy. The happy graduates said, "Lissy, we'll be back next year to celebrate when you graduate after your fifth year with your MBA!"

"OMG! Look how he's looking at you," said another friend.

"Who Girl!" said Lisette.

"That Alex Cooper! I didn't know he was a fifth year graduate too," said Lisette's friend. Her friends all started laughing.

Lisette wanted to know, "What is so funny?"

One of her friends stopped laughing long enough to respond: "That dude has been asking you out for the past four years, and you've always told him no. Why don't you go and congratulate him." To her friends' surprise, Lisette said, "Okay." Lisette went over to Alex Cooper and said," Congratulations." He said, "Thank you. Would you come to the party that my parents are giving me later this evening?" To his surprise, Lisette said, "Yes." The rest, as they often say, is history . . .

Alex Cooper had done what no other man had been able to do for Lisette Donavan: he changed her thwarted definition of love. Lisette found that being in love with Alex heightened her every sense—the sky was more vividly blue, the rain drops smelled fresher . . . the world, in general, had more pleasant sensations. This was the strangest thing that Lisette had ever felt.

Alex was looking at Lisette strangely. "Why are you looking at me that way?" Lisette asked.

Alex responded by saying, "'Cause."

"'Cause what?"

"Lisette, it's no secret that I've dated a lot of girls."

"So ... are we bragging now? Why do you think I waited so long to say "yes" to a date with you?" Lisette responded, somewhat perturbed.

"Please let me finish. I was about to say . . . you are so different. You're not just a pretty face with a fine body."

Lisette interrupted, "So you're just looking at my body . . . is that it?"

"Lisette, let me say what I have to say!" Then in a much gentler, endearing tone, Alex said, "Please?"

With her eyes, Lisette said go on.

"Your beautiful face and body . . . that's just the sweet icing on the cake. But your inside, your mind, your determination, the way you set goals, how you love your family. Heck! Even the way you love animals and help strays. You didn't date me, but I watched you for a long time. I knew you were smart, like me." Alex laughed.

Lisette chided him again. "I said don't be a braggart. Okay, Alex, that's enough. Confession time. I had you checked out to see what kind of person you were and what your grades were like, and I had been watching you too, brother, from the corner of my eyes." They both laughed until they were crying.

Lisette and Alex became quite a hot number. Of course, Alex promised that he would be patient with Lisette and allow her to focus on school to maintain her 3.98 average. With this kind of average, Alex told Lisette that she may be able to get a fellowship to an Ivy League law School, just as he was hoping to do. Alex decided to work for a Fortune 500 firm until Lisette finished her fifth year, then they would both go to an Ivy League Law school together as Mr. and Mrs. Alexander Cooper. They started researching which schools they would send applications to. Lisette and Alex became engaged as she was entering her fifth year. Her mother was so excited and had started planning Lisette's wedding so that she would graduate with her MBA one weekend and then come home for her wedding the next weekend.

Her father said, "Hey, I'm finally getting my second son."

Cindi said, "Finally, I've graduated from bridesmaid to maid of honor." You would have thought that Alex would have chosen one of his other frat brothers as best man, but he chose Lisette's brother, Andy. They became close when Lisette's brother, Andy, pledged a fraternity of which Alex was the Dean of Pledgees.

Lisette tried to stay focused on her studies. She and Alex had a goal that they called *their American Dream*. With Alex so far away working, it became more and more difficult to focus and this feeling was so unfamiliar to Lisette. She often found herself wondering what Alex was doing with his spare time and even wondered how he staved off advances from attractive women that he worked with. She had never been unsure of herself or been the jealous type and Alex assured her that he had met the perfect woman.

Lisette would retort with, "There is no perfect woman . . . no perfect human being, so you can take that two-cent flattery to some other dumb bunny." Alex would laugh and say, "Well, in Lisette Donavan, I've found a woman that's as close as possible to my definition of the perfect woman." Since their engagement, Alex had convinced Lisette that it was okay for them to express their love sexually. Lisette was Alex's sweet virgin, and he was so gentle with her, yet powerful. Alex made lovemaking everything and more than she had dreamed it would be.

Alex came south twice a month to see Lisette and his family. Whenever Lisette could get a break from her studies and wedding planning, which wasn't often, she would go north to visit Alex. One of the months in which Alex was supposed to come to visit Lisette, he was inundated with a lot of overtime at work and could not get away. In addition, the weather was extremely bad.

Lisette told her Mom, "I hate getting hooked on a man. I miss Alex so much."

Her Mom said, "Baby, it's not getting hooked—it's called being in love. You'll learn how to put it all in perspective. You've always been so level-headed. I don't see you acting crazy or neglecting school or other priorities just because you're in love and engaged."

"Thanks, Mom, for your confidence in me. Lately, I haven't had as much confidence in myself as I usually do."

"Honey, don't ever second guess yourself. You are a very bright young lady and you have a fine young man who will soon be your husband. Now stop worrying. Let me see my old confident Lisette."

Then Lisette's Mom leaned over and hugged her with that comforting, healing hug that always seemed to make her feel so much better and so loved.

Lisette didn't really like flying in bad weather, and it was snowing pretty badly. The plane had to circle for nearly thirty minutes before landing. There were so many planes in a holding pattern because it took time to keep the tarmac cleared off. This really wasn't a good time to travel. The snow had even reached the south and closed down the university, which gave Lisette extra time to get ahead with her graduate work and plan a surprise trip to be with her "Boo."

She and Alex could keep each other warm and stay under the electric blanket, romancing each other for the next two days. Lisette was thinking: *Alex will probably think I'm crazy travelling in a snow storm when everyone was told to stay inside. But he'll also be happy as a 'kid in a candy factory' to have his almost perfect girl with him to weather the storm with.* Lisette had it all thought out, whispering to herself as she deplaned, "I'll pick up a few of our favorite snacks and get to Alex's apartment."

Lisette wondered all the way while riding in the cab whether she would get to Alex's apartment alive. There was an accident on every corner and cars were slipping and sliding everywhere, barely missing her cab. Lisette asked the cabby, "Why do you do this for a living?" The cabby replied, "I got a family to support." Lisette paid the cabby extra and prayed he would be able to get home safely to his family in this snow storm.

Lisette was consumed with excitement and ready to pounce on Alex. This would be the best surprise gift that she had ever given him. Lisette walked into the apartment. She could hear their favorite love-making music coming from Alex's room. Lisette thought to herself, *Alex misses me so much, he's playing our music.* Lisette could feel herself becoming very aroused so she started taking off her clothes and only kept on her new lacy, sexy teddy for Alex to take off. She was proud of her shapely, five-four, 110 pound frame with her firm legs and arms from running.

She just knew that one look at her in that new teddy would send Alex soaring and have him groping all over her. She could already feel his strong hands running through her soft hair. She thought of his soft, full lips, and majestic tongue, and could no longer contain her thirst and desire for her man. She felt so sensuous and knew she would give her man whatever he wanted. Lisette slowly walked into Alex's room and smelled their incense, which only titillated her more; but then she was stunned by Alex's naked upper muscular body moving rhythmically and heard his deep sexy voice crooning into the ear of another woman.

Lisette heard Alex say in a low and deep voice, "You are my perfect woman."

The woman responded, "Yes, yes...I am."

"That's right baby . . . you know who you are . . . my perfect woman."

Lisette, in a daze, quietly backed out of the bedroom and methodically put on her clothes. She went to Alex's kitchen and without thinking, looked for the sharpest knife that she could find, returned to the bedroom and without a word, as Alex and his perfect woman were about to climax, Lisette, with all her strength, began thrusting the knife into Alex's back.

The Officer said, "Mr. and Mrs. Donavan, this way, please."

"When can we see her?" Mrs. Donavan kept asking. "I need to see my daughter."

The Officer replied, "Your daughter has been charged with attempted murder. She stabbed the young man over ten times. It's a miracle that he's alive. You may not be able to see her until arraignment."

Mrs. Donavan started crying. Mr. Donavan held his wife and said, "Honey please, we must be strong for Lisette now."

The Officer asked, "Mr. Donavan, do you have an attorney for your daughter?"

"Why, yes, we do. He's flying in, but there's been some hold up with him getting here because of the weather."

"Honey, I remember a conversation I had with Lisette a few months before this tragic incident with Alex where she felt like she was losing control."

Mr. Donavan said, "Baby, you know I am just so grateful, that out of his guilt, humanity or whatever it was, Alex pleaded with the courts to have the charges against Lisette dropped, which left her with a criminal record, but no jail time. I think sending her to New York to be with her great aunt away from all this was the best thing for her for now. The attorney found a great therapist that I think Lisette will like. So let's just try to concentrate on the positive."

"So whatcha doing after work today, Lissy . . . running in Central Park or taking another on-line class?" Hattie asked laughing. "Girl you still searching for the *American Dream* aren't you?" she asked.

Lisette replied, "Are you kidding . . . the *American Dream* is just a pipe dream."

17. Lisette Donavan's American Dream, Cheryl B. Williams, clbwms@gmail.com

18.

Diary of a Sneaky Woman

Michael D. Beckford

A cold winter's morning breezed by a slender five-eight, 135 pound, Puerto Rican woman. She wasn't the only woman running late on the mean streets of New York City.

"Taxi, taxi!" the woman yelled out, as her hair took a whiplash from the cool mornings' breeze. An officer and a gentleman approached the woman with a tempered curiosity; his mind drizzled with the thought of her in his arms. He quickly flashed back to reality when he realized that the Puerto Rican woman was running on a sidewalk full of streaming people. The officer caught up with the mysterious woman, now only ten feet in front of him. She barely noticed his approach as she anxiously yelled once more for a cab on the busy New York City streets.

"Hey there, little lady, what's your name?" The officer looked on in glee; his eyes took a splash of one thousand pictures per second, each picture noting every curve, her piercing dimples, jet black hair, and her plush black eyes. She was dressed in her usual black and white uniform.

"My name is Lisette Donavan, and I don't mean to be rude, Mr. Officer, but I'm late for work. My cab is waiting for me."

"Yes, I see. You just about walked over three people. I'll let you go this time, but I'll certainly have to give you a citation the next time." The officer looked at Lisette more intimately, still taking pictures and eyeing areas he shouldn't. What he didn't notice was Lisette's change in composure; a moment of tension filled her blood stream as the thought of a citation would truly open up a box of secrets she wouldn't be proud of.

Just as the officer finished his last word with Lisette, she vanished into the taxi.

"Take me to the corner of Fifth and Eighth, Pappy. And hurry up. I'm late." With a sigh of relief, she exhaled.

"Ms. Lisette Donavan, you are always late." The man's blank stare said everything his lips couldn't.

"I'm sorry, sir. Traffic was a female dog." She held her composure, neither confirming nor denying the man's allegations.

"What?" Her boss's shoulders drew up in defense.

"Never mind, sir. You'll get it on the way out." She silently laughed to herself, knowing that this stuck up millionaire wouldn't understand a joke if Bernie Mac rose up out of his grave and said it to the man himself.

"Ok, Lisette, but this is the last time you can be late. The wife is upstairs panicking because the kids haven't been fed. And to make matters worse, she said that she spotted some crumbs in the room where the kids play. I'll tell you this, Miss Donavan. You better pray to your god that my wife hasn't dialed a number out of that yellow phone book of hers upstairs."

"Ok, sir. I got it all under control." Every curse word imaginable flashed through her mind. "I'm going to fix the kids some breakfast and clean up those unbiblical crumbs," she sarcastically remarked while dangling the two most visible fruits of God's creation for her boss to take notice, a stunt she liked to pull often to get men to change the subject.

His composure was unchanged.

"Ok, do what you have to do. I'm gone for business. By the way, my wife has your check, so be nice." A whisper of a devilish smile lasting all of five seconds seeped deeply in the millionaire's facial features.

Dudley Brown grew up on the mean streets of Harlem, a renaissance man of sorts. His mother's finances, or lack thereof, drove them to live in the projects. They adored Section Eight living and worshipped food stamps; it was a common staple for his community.

The projects taught Dudley Brown a lot about business. As a matter of fact, it was indeed a playground of sorts for Dudley to conceptualize his future business dealings as an entrepreneur. For Dudley, the projects taught him a lot about timing, customer service, and what happens when a deal goes bad. Everyone knew when the cops made their rounds; and everyone especially knew when the dope man came around to collect. Dudley's lust for money was more powerful than his peers' lust for women.

"Mrs. Brown, I'm so, so sorry for being late. It was a train wreck of traffic outside. I have grits, bacon, and toast ready for the kids." Lisette smiled, hoping to win favor with a confused looking Mrs. Brown.

"You might as well throw that away," she said. "Lissy, the kids are late for school because of you." She picked up steam. "They don't have time to eat grits, toast, or bacon. Meanwhile, I saw some crumbs in their video game room this morning, Miss Donavan. Any reason why crumbs would still be in that room?" Her fury could be heard downstairs where the kids were getting their backpacks ready.

With a deep breath, Lisette held her composure. "I'm sure the kids could have left crumbs after I had already cleaned that room."

Mrs. Brown fired back. "My kids know not to eat in any of their rooms. You call yourself a maid! All you do is sashay your Puerto Rican booty in my house, leaving your scent for my husband to smell. Are you sleeping with my husband, Lisette?" she demanded while fanning herself with Lisette's check.

Lisette's face was flushed, and her fists were cupped. She reminisced on the one mistake that caused her to flee her home country of Puerto Rico because of her anger. As quickly as it came, the not-so-distant memory evaporated and her anger subsided. She unclenched her fists and her facial features once more revealed that of a runway model.

Lisette responded. "No, I'm not screwing your husband, Mrs. Brown. I've said this for the thousandth time."

The 21 Lives of Lisette Donavan   153

"That's probably why he pays you $3,500 a month. You doing my husband some special favors? My mother was a maid in a small town in Georgia. The most money she ever brought home in a month was a thousand dollars to feed five mouths—three girls and two boys.

"We had a no-good something for a father. A 'sperm donor,' the kids call it these days. That man barely put a grain of corn on the table while my mama went around cleaning for those white rich people in their luxury homes. She might as well have been a slave; she worked more hours than a firefighter. She busted her tail up six in the morning and back home at nine o'clock at night."

"I told myself, I couldn't live that kind of life. That's why I got me a rich man, and you are not going to take him away from me. You ain't the only one that got special gifts from God, you know."

After a long day's work at *Fevor Magazine,* which Dudley Brown owned, he returned home a little unsettled from the events that took place earlier in the morning.

"Hey, honey." Dudley tiptoed into their plush Manhattan condo around ten at night. A whisp of perfume emanated from the shoulder of his polished, Italian-threaded, custom suit made just right for his six-two, 245 pound frame. Many of the ladies confused him with Taye Diggs because they both had those thick black eyebrows, a Mr. Clean shaven head, and a smile that could put a toxic spell on even his worst enemies.

"So, did you fire Lissy?" Dudley hustled up the stairs trying to get away from his wife. He didn't want that familiar scent to enter her nostrils.

"No, I didn't fire her. The poor girl looked sad. She reminded me of my crazy mother. She'd do anything to keep a check coming."

By the time Mrs. Brown had finished speaking, Dudley had already availed himself of the master bedroom shower. He didn't hear a word she said. He was happily covered in Irish Spring suds and prepared to rinse after five minutes.

"Dudley, why did you come here so late tonight? I made dinner for us. You said that you'd be here three hours ago." Little did Mrs. Brown know, Dudley was already upstairs, out of the shower, and ready for bed. Her approaching argument would just have to wait for the morning.

"I love you, baby," Dudley whispered. He dimmed the lights.

"I—uh—love you, too." She stuttered, frustrated with her husband. "Goodnight."

Waking up to the sounds of horns and chirping birds, Ashley Brown was agitated. Her feelings of insecurity were ready to blow right from under her.

"So, Dudley, who was it last night?" She let loose.

"What do you mean? What are you talking about, Ashley?" He looked for a suit to wear for work.

"I'm talking about one of them skanks you done been with. You think I didn't smell that odd perfume on your coat again? What's up, Dudley? Are you screwing the maid, too?" Her fury woke the kids.

Dudley jumped out of the closet, "No, I'm not screwing the maid! Now leave me alone. I've got work to do. You know somebody has to pay for those ten-thousand dollar bracelets on your arm."

"That's a low blow. I'm done. Just because you own a multi-million dollar magazine doesn't mean that I have to bow down to you. I have my degree as well. I chose to stay home with the kids."

"Hey honey. I have to go to work and I don't know what you are talking about." He raced down the stairs and was startled by Listette's presence half-way to the first floor. "Hey. When did you get here?" A look of surprise overshadowed his frustration.

"I told you that I'm trying to be here on time, sir. You forgot that I have a key." She smirked.

The 21 Lives of Lisette Donavan   155

"No, no. Handle your business. My wife is a little . . ." He whispered something in her ear.

"Ha! Ha!" She laughed hysterically. "I feel the same way Mr. Brown, the same way."

"Well, I'm off to work now. Have a great day, Lissy." He cheered up a bit.

"Yes, you, too," She said with a subtle wink, barely traveling at the speed of sound.

"Dudley, is that you downstairs? What are you doing? You come right back up here immediately. We still have some talking to do." Ashley broke down. Her head met her hands in another episode of *who wants to be a miserable wife*. Ashley couldn't stand the thought of losing her husband to another woman. She loved that man like Kobe Bryant loved the game of basketball. It would be devastating both mentally and financially to lose him.

"No, Mrs. Brown. It's me downstairs. Your husband just left," Lisette somberly remarked. All the hate in the world couldn't mask the pain that she too felt for Mrs. Ashley Brown, for this cycle of events had been taking place since her arrival with the Brown family two years ago.

Two years ago, life was a lot different for Lisette. She was just finishing up her Bachelors in Journalism and working one dead beat job after another. She was so proud of herself. The life she left in Puerto Rico was now far behind her, but the memory of that one ill-conceived day could never leave her—the day that her sister lost her innocence to an opportunistic private in the U.S. Military stationed in Puerto Rico.

What happened to her sister, Lucita, on the twenty-first day of September had been the key to Lisette's secret box stored in her heart. That day in 2009 began with Lucita knocked out when Private Green unlocked the hotel door. He met an unresponsive Lucita on her bed while she was in a deep sleep. He being young, only twenty-years old and ready to do anything that came his way, unzipped her pants to see if she would move. She was still unresponsive. Then he started at her shirt, her bra, her underwear. She still didn't budge, so he went further. His mind had already played out the dirty deeds he would do to her, and in fifteen minutes it was over. Blood was shed all over her bed. He broke her seal and she woke up screaming. Before Private Green could react, Lucita had already run out the door naked, pleading for help. The hotel guests looked at her in fear, with all the blood seeping down her legs. They assumed she had been shot.

"Llamar a alguien de la Policía,".the hotel steward said. He repeated once more, "Someone call the police."

Lucita ran around the lobby frantically and trembling. Finally, one of the hotel employees had sense enough to give her a towel to cover up.

"The ambulance is on its way."

"Gracias." Lucita nervously gestured to the strange man (the hotel steward?).

"Hey, do you have a name or someone you can call?"

"Sí, mi hermana, quiero llamar a mi hermana." She spoke to him very briskly.

"You want to call your sister. Ok, what's her number?"

"Enfermos marcar su." Lucita said rapidly, still shaking from the fear and anxiety placed on her by Private Green.

"Ok, go right ahead. Dial her. I hear the sound of the ambulance now." The receptionist sighed with relief. Forgetting to ask some of the pertinent questions.

Private Green was already gone. He'd slipped down the back stairway, running through town yelling for the nearest taxi. Meanwhile, Listette was on the phone with Lucita, struggling to decipher all that had transpired.

"Wait a minute, wait a minute. What did you say happened to you?" Lisette screamed over the phone.

"I believe that I was raped." Lucita voiced to her sister.

"Mam, you are going to have to get off the phone. We are here to help you. We need to take you to the hospital," one of the paramedics gestured.

"It's my sister," Lucita yelled back at the paramedic in frustration.

Calmly, the paramedic said, "Tell your sister that we will be at the Ashford Hospital."

"Si," Lucita screamed and hung up the phone, leaving Listette in limbo.

After arriving at the hospital, Lisette received the full story and a good description of Private Green. Under the cover of darkness, a few yards from Fort Buchanan, Lisette waited for Private Green to exit the base. To her delight, she found him. She plotted to kill him, using her body as a weapon of choice to attract him. She properly executed her plan by brutally wounding his genitals and stabbing him in the heart. She laid him to rest in the woods nearby where he bled to death.

Two years later, Lisette showed up in New York, right at the desk of Mr. Dudley Brown looking for a job as an intern with *Fevor Magazine*. Although she had the backing of a Bachelors Degree, it was still very hard to find work in a frail economy and the print business constantly bellying up due to the Internet.

"I'm sorry, Miss. Donavan. We are no longer accepting interns, but I will double your pay with benefits to work as a maid at my house." He wooed her with such charm and swagger, she said yes before she even realized what she had consented to at the time.

Meanwhile, U.S. Marshals were on her tail, following lead after lead to find the brazen woman who killed a United States Marine only a few yards from the base. When the Marshalls discovered that she was long gone from Puerto Rico and in the U.S. mainland, they increased the bounty. They finally received a tip that she was using the alias of Lisette Donavan in the states, instead of her real name, Catina Rodriguez, the name her mother and two siblings knew her by.

Two years ago, a lot had changed for Lisette, but her jet black hair, tender body, and seductive ways had all stayed the same. Waking herself from memory lane, Lisette returned upstairs to tend to Mrs. Brown.

"Mrs. Brown, Dudley is an interesting man, but I don't believe he's going to leave you. He has too much at stake if he does. Besides, you will get fifty percent of what he owns anyway, so what's there to worry about?"

Mrs. Brown turned around in shock. "Why are you telling me this, Lisette?"

"I'm just trying to prevent one woman from being taken advantage of by another man. That's all, no harm intended." She smiled, as her day was done at the Brown's home. She walked downstairs, checked her keys and noticed the heavy scent of an odd perfume lingering from the kitchen.

"Agent Ron, looks like we got her." A U.S. Marshall was waiting outside at the front door while the other was in the kitchen.

"Agent Wanda, are you sure that is Catina Rodriguez?"

"I am sure, sir. She may be a little older now, but her facial features haven't changed a bit—every curve, her piercing dimples, jet black hair, and her plush black eyes. This is Catina Rodriguez."

"Put on the handcuffs." Wanda swooped from around the kitchen corner, looking at the back of a steadily paced Lisette. Breathing heavy and labored, Wanda finally caught Lisette before she exited the back door. "Catina Rodriguez, you are under arrest for the senseless murder of Private Malcolm Green."

18. Diary of a Sneaky Woman, Michael Beckford,
   michaeldbeckford@gmail.com

19.

The Snake

Kenneth E. Taite

Lisette Donavan rose from a restless sleep, aghast, and visibly shaken—this was her normal morning routine. No need to invest in an alarm clock as guilt and fear were sufficient harbingers of the dawn. After a quick self-pat down, Lisette blinked her eyes and held them open, bringing the room into focus with the attenuated sounds of the Brooklyn, New York, streetscape bustling below.

She breathed a sigh of relief with the understanding that last night's particularly hellish nightmare was just that—a dream. But her reprieve was short-lived as she realized, yet again, that she was a woman on the run with no home, no identity, and no past.

She rose, casting a long silhouetted image of her lean but curvy size eight frame against her sun-washed bedroom wall. She transitioned into a ten-minute exercise routine followed by a quick shower, a cream cheese bagel for breakfast, and a swallow of orange juice. Her morning routine was never complete without checking her appearance in the full-length hallway mirror next to the front door as she left.

"Something's wrong . . . but what?" Lisette mumbled. Her eyes scanned the mirror's reflection from head to toe making sure that she looked the part of . . . No! That she **was** Suzette Ortiz, proud owner and operator of Ortiz Cleaning and Wash and Fold Service.

She noticed something about her appearance that just wasn't right—it was her roots. Her straight auburn hair was giving way to her naturally curly dark-brown locks.

"Ughhh! This can't be happening now, I've got to catch the 8:15! I've gotta go!" She leaned her head down closer to the mirror for a more thorough examination. Her appearance was critical for her survival, thus her obsession with it. The uniform was fine, Dominican accent, and back-story, "Check!" But the hair was just not right.

Lisette was as meticulous as she was paranoid. She was convinced that the only reason she had been able to elude capture for so long was because of her three principles: Caution, detail, and consistency. With the ever present fear of losing focus and breaking routine, Lisette's subconscious provided perpetual graphic reminders of the consequences. Her reoccurring nightmares warned her of this every night without fail.

The dreams started with her at rest, content, and vulnerable. As was her nature, she was open to her environment and anxious to take in the local flavor, be a woman of the community, and grow roots to be successful, have a career, marriage, and kids. Then, there was a sound, a feeling, a certain disquiet that overcame her— a warning. She started to run, leaving her former situation behind. She took nothing with her as she knew it would just slow her down. The snake was coming...

It was a ravenous prehistoric-looking creature of uncanny size, intelligence, and stamina. Dark, dull, and flat in color, it blended into the shadows. Its only sheen was in its bulbous, metallic eyes, so big they shined like headlights. She began to run from this massive being, but the snake was relentless; not limited by terrain or barriers of any kind. Like water it found the least path of resistance by circumvention or breaking through. It could not be retarded or bargained with—it was a force of nature. Like an old weighty clipper ship it moved slowly, but what it lacked in speed it made up in stamina and a myopic focus on its prey. It never stopped or slowed below its current pace. The serpent didn't sleep nor did it slumber. Lisette had seen the wide gulf disappear between herself and the snake night after night. If the dream was a dependable omen, succumbing to this beast was inevitable. But with her sheer determination and God's grace, Lisette had changed her reality before.

Now back to those pesky roots . . .

She tore into the cramped narrow hall closet, looking for . . . "Could it be . . . did I put it back where I could find it this time . . . Yes! Thank you, God!"

Lisette uncovered her trusty wig that she had picked up along the way from West Virginia; she aptly named it "the life saver." She freshened up the wig and positioned it on her head, leaning into the mirror again to check her appearance.

"I could do better if I had time, but I can pull this off for today at least," she spoke to the mirror's reflection. Sensing the lateness of the hour, Lisette grabbed her small overnight bag and her personal music player for her commute into Manhattan.

Today was Friday, one of Lisette's two favorite days including Monday. On Monday's and Friday's, she worked the Herring account. This account was not her most lucrative and the work wasn't the easiest to do, but it was the client that gave her butterflies at the mere thought of his name . . . Michael C. Herring, Esquire. Lisette liked to say his name as it appeared on the plaques and documents lining his midtown flat. He was everything she had ever dreamed of in a man—six-four, 218 pounds of chiseled, olive-complexion, humanity with a baby face, and a blinding white smile for good measure.

But there's more . . .

Herring was different from most of the Manhattan lawyers and well-heeled big shots for whom Lisette worked. The requisite egotism and haughtiness were replaced by a quiet self-confidence and humility. She could say this with assurance as she had dozens of clients in the five boroughs, Connecticut, and Northern New Jersey. In the eighteen months that she had been working for Michael Herring, their relationship had slowly evolved from being strictly professional to relaxed, bordering on intimate.

Michael fell in love with Lisette on the first day she came to work for him. It was her eyes, large and almond-shaped, framed in long dark lashes. They held her pain, passion, and desire for a better life. Mystified as to why such an intelligent and beautiful woman was unmarried and cleaning his toilets and floors twice weekly, soon the small talk became more probing. Michael soon realized that his attempts to get to know Lisette better were off-putting to her. Lisette viewed his aloof questioning as more of a deposition than a friendly chat. In spite of all of his redeeming qualities, she remained steadfast to her three principles . . . for a time.

"I apologize, Miss Ortiz. I just find you so fascinating," Michael pleaded.

"Oh, I see, fascinating until you have had your way with me, and there is nothing else left to your imagination?" Lisette countered defensively.

"No! Please forgive me if I am being too forward. Normally, I would not ask these things, but I *really* like you. I just want to know everything about the *real* you. I don't know how else to prove it to you," Michael persisted.

Michael's last response sent a chill down Lisette's spine; she was torn in two pieces. In her mind she was rejoicing at the prospect of being with the finest man that she had ever known in her twenty-eight years of living. But at the same time, she had to consider the consequences of being discovered before she could clear her name. Lisette yearned to share her true feelings for Michael but knew that it would be to her detriment.

"I like you to Michael . . . excuse me . . . Mr. Herring, but as a client."

Michael wanted to shrink and run out of his own apartment from the sheer embarrassment of rejection. But he was a gentleman, and a man of proper breeding though his sheepish grin couldn't be helped, he managed to straighten himself up and leave for work. "Ok, I understand, Miss Ortiz; I just wanted you to know that I am one of the good guys. But my offer to have lunch sometime is open-ended."

As Michael opened the door to leave, Lisette breathlessly responded, "Thank you for understanding, Mr. Herring. Once I get to know you better, maybe we can make it dinner."

SCREEEEECHHH!!! Lisette was jostled out of her flashback by the turbulence of the subway car. *"Just ten more minutes,"* she thought. The usually unpleasant commute into the city was the worst part of her day, but this was no ordinary day.

The 21 Lives of Lisette Donavan

Last week, Michael mustered the courage to ask Lisette out on a date, to which she promptly accepted. The two mutually agreed that they would both take off work and spend the day together. It had been over a year since he first professed his feelings for her, and by now, she was fully disarmed.

Lisette began to read a remnant of the New York Daily News that was crumbled on the empty seat beside her to pass the time before her stop arrived. She was unaware of the front page story facing away from her titled, *"Patricidal Appalachian Fem on the Lamb in NYC."*

Michael knew about her past—all of it. For the past year, he had spared no expense to research and cross-reference bits of information that he was able to glean from her with the fugitive and missing persons records of ten eastern states. Today, he planned to confront her with this information.

By now, Lisette had reached her subway stop, a half block from Michael's apartment. She had a peace about her that had eluded her for years. A quiet calm inhabited her soul as if to say, "It's alright, child." More calming than the day she arrived in New York City, penniless, hungry, and gaunt—the result of her 400-mile forced-march from West Virginia. As she gazed upon the Manhattan skyline, illuminated by the low-hanging sun, she cried tears of joy.

She was free.

Free from Jake Donavan's reckless descent from loving husband and doting father to drug-addled wife beater and abusive father to Lisette and her older sister for over seven years. Free from the voracious mob that formed shortly after the discovery of her father's rotted corpse in the family mineral mine.

Lisette began to ascend the long stairwell from the subway onto the street above. Step by step, the warmth of the morning sun slowly washed over her head first. She was convinced, *"I'm going to open up to him today."*

At this point, she needed no further reassurance, just a plan. Lisette had contemplated this for weeks. She had even come up with an explanation for the Suzette Ortiz alias. "It's a back story for my business. New Yorkers love Hispanic housekeepers. They think that they're getting more bang for the buck . . . " As lame as it sounded, Lisette was willing to try anything in order to come out from her shadowy existence, even if it meant being someone else for the rest of her life. *"First an identity—any name will do—just as long as eventually the last name is Herring."* Lisette sprang from the subway stairs and into the flow of sidewalk foot traffic. Her focus totally on a future with Michael, she didn't hear the appeals of her fellow sidewalk mates for her to speed up or move. She didn't feel the pushing and shoving of busy pedestrians trying to beat the stroke of 9:00 A.M. She didn't notice the heavy police presence surrounding Michael's apartment building either.

So much for the three principles.

Still in a cloud of amorous bliss, Lisette greeted the doorman to Michael's building. "Buenos Dias, Raul."

Raul, the doorman, only spoke to her with his eyes. If she was paying attention she would have gotten his message—"RUN!" Instead, she ascended the lobby stairs with a spritely bounce to Michael's fourth floor apartment.

Lisette thought it strange that the normally bustling apartment building seemed empty and quiet. Lisette reached the fourth floor landing and stopped in her tracks. Suddenly, her subconscious mind replayed the images that she had just witnessed but not paid attention to until now. *"The NYPD was surrounding the building, Raul was acting strangely, the building was empty— THE SNAKE!"*

Lisette's uncanny nightmare had finally manifested itself into reality. It was time to pay for the unspeakable sin of killing her father, Jake Donavan, that ogre who had so callously stolen her innocence. Her mind and body were no longer her own as pure adrenaline took over.

Lisette darted back into the stairwell from whence she came. As a phalanx of uniformed law enforcement officers clumsily marched up from the third floor, a plain-clothed detective hurriedly descended down the stairwell from the upper floors. The trap was sprung and there was no way out now. Lisette managed to make it to the fifth floor landing; she would have to make her stand there, as law enforcement were directly above and below. As she forced herself into the hallway, she traversed the hall with purpose. As she made it to the middle of the long corridor near the bank of elevators, she assessed her scant options. For the moment, the stomping and the clanging of the officers' footsteps in the stairwells was not audible, but she knew that there was a debt to be paid, and that snake was coming.

Suddenly, the door opened to apartment 507, and an old blue-haired lady ambled out of the apartment with a small fluffy dog stuffed in her $4,000 designer carry bag. She didn't notice Lisette standing in front of her and was oblivious to the events of the morning.

"Time to do the business, time to do the business," the old lady sang as she showed a Pooper-Scooper to the diminutive canine. Before the lady could close her door, the police poured into the hallway from all directions.

"FREEZE! FREEZE!"

Lisette did the opposite. She tapped the old lady on her right shoulder and slipped into her apartment on the left side as the lady turned to see who tapped her.

"I'm so sorry," Lisette offered remorsefully as she locked out the old lady. Lisette made haste to the exterior patio; it was connected to a fire escape. As she threw her leg over the railing, she felt the intense vibration of dozens of footsteps shaking and rattling the precarious red iron structure. By then the front door of 507 was forced open by the police.

The snake was advancing from all sides . . .

Their standard issue service revolvers shined like the fangs of the snake in Lisette's dreams.

"It's not my fault!" Lisette screamed repeatedly as she straddled the railing of the fire escape.

"I know it's not! You were defending yourself and your family!" cried out a familiar voice from the threshold of 507. It was Michael Herring, flanked by Lisette's mother, sister, Jacqueline, and brother, Jacob. Jr. "They have been looking for you for years, Lisette. You are not a criminal—I can help you through this process," Michael continued.

"I don't believe you! You lied to me and brought the police! I didn't mean to hurt my father, but I couldn't take him doing those things to Jackie and me anymore," she explained desperately. Lisette's mother and sister began to sob and plead for her to get down from the rail before she fell five stories to her death.

"I love you, Lisette Donavan! I love the *real* you," proclaimed Michael as he eased his way to the patio in an effort to not provoke her. "I knew there was something special about you from the first time we met. But what I didn't know until recently was how strong you are, how brave you are, and how deep your love is for the ones *you* love." Michael motioned for her family to join him on the patio.

Lisette was speechless; it was too much information to process in the span of twenty minutes. Earlier this morning, she was contemplating spending a romantic day with Michael and taking in all that Manhattan had to offer for once. Now she found herself making a decision to turn herself in and face murder charges or jump and end it all.

In her heart she knew that the four people that shared the patio with her were sincere; they loved her. That's why she made that terrible sacrifice so many years ago. It was for them.

Lisette thought that the snake that haunted her in her dreams was a subconscious manifestation of the police, bounty hunters, and cronies of her father hell-bent on making her pay for what she had done. At this moment, she realized that it was the guilt that she had saddled herself down with for so many years. She was heavy-laden with a crippling ignominy that she could repress in the conscious world but not escape in the subliminal.

As her panicked countenance was now overcome by a spirit of peace, she locked eyes with Michael and smiled as if to say. *"It's time to let go."* Lisette surveyed her situation one final time. After looking up and down at the police on the fire escape above and below her, Lisette scanned the room, noticing the dozens of people in the background behind Michael and her family. She took a deep breath and leered at the bustle of yellow cabs, tour buses, and pedestrians scrambling beneath her. Then, she stared into

Michael's earnest eyes for what seemed like an eternity and extended her hand to him.

Michael whisked her off of the railing in one swoop as they transitioned into a long kiss, something that had eluded them for many months.

"I promise that I will take care of you," Michael whispered as they locked in a full embrace.

"You have done so much for me already," Lisette replied.

19. The Snake: Kenneth E. Taite, kennethtaite@gmail.com

20.

Double D Death

Felicia S.W. Thomas

Lissy was sick of hearing it. She heard it from people on the train. She heard it walking down the street. She'd even overheard people at work saying it. Lisette Donavan was a beautiful twenty-eight year old woman, educated, and a lot of fun. But no one saw that. All people talked about and commented on was her most prominent feature—her enormous breasts.

"Look, man, she got two brains!" she inevitably heard at least once a week.

Ta-tas, headlights, hooters, knockers, jugs—whatever euphemism there was for breasts, Lissy had heard it. Oddly enough, people didn't see all of her. Her five-three, 240 pound frame was hard to miss, but she managed to be invisible.

Invisible, even in New York City. She worked in one of New York City's most elegant hotels, as a maid. It was humiliating. She had a B.S. degree in Journalism, but she could never get a job in her field. She was terrific on paper—above average intelligence, prestigious internships, and glowing letters of recommendation. In person, however, she was treated like a sideshow freak at a poor man's circus. She'd interviewed for positions at newspapers around the country. She dressed smartly— careful not to draw too much attention to her chest. She dazzled with sparkling conversation and her inside knowledge of the industry.

It didn't matter, though. If the interviewer was a man, she couldn't have done herself a greater disservice if she sat there in filthy overalls blowing spit bubbles. They obviously didn't hear a word she said and their eyes never strayed above her neckline. Lissy recognized that look too often. The women were discreetly nasty, but the men couldn't, or wouldn't, hide their disgust. It brought back memories of her beautiful, slim, older sister and athletic, younger brother, making fun of her—calling her fat every chance they got.

After a solid year of interviews, her last being at a small New York City paper, and no offers, she decided she had to work somewhere. The hotel where she'd been staying for that last interview was hiring, they had a uniform that fit her 40DDs, and they weren't scared away by her criminal record.

With great difficulty, Lissy tolerated the verbal abuse. She did her work as quickly and efficiently as possible, with as little interaction with guests, as possible. The minority of guests just ignored her, but the majority had to make it known they saw her and didn't like what they saw. The worst offenders were the handsome men. They treated her like a disposable wipe—used her up and tossed her away. Although she wore a name tag, they seldom used her name.

"Hey, you there," the three-piece suits would say. "Bring me some more towels and have these shoes shined and . . .," Never a please or a thank you, and she had to suffer such degradation for minimum wage and few tips.

"That's a nice tie you're wearing." Still, she tried to be nice and engage them in conversation, but they would take out their cell phones and start talking before she was even finished. They would look at her face, as if to say, "How dare you even speak to me," drop to her gigantic chest, and then look away. Lissy was sick of feeling like garbage. Her tolerance level had peaked. After three years of hoarding tips and nursing a collection of hurts, she finally decided to end her misery.

Lissy arrived at home around four one morning. Before going into her own apartment, she banged twice on the door of her neighbor, Sammy Berry. It took Sammy five minutes to get to the door and remove the seven locks he had on it. Lissy and Sammy lived across the hall from each other on the seventh floor of a nine-story, dilapidated building that looked condemned from the outside and was located squarely in the middle of a crime-ridden neighborhood.

"Hold on, Lissy! I'm coming!" Sammy growled. "I know the building ain't on fire. I don't smell no smoke." When he opened the door, the lone light bulb in the one-room apartment cast a dim shadow on Lissy's exhausted countenance. Lissy looked into the world-weary, fifty-year old face of Sammy, who sported salt and pepper dreadlocks, and who wore sunglasses at night.

"How did you know it was me, Sammy?" Lissy asked. "It could have been your friend, Rufus."

"That perfume, girl. Got to cost you a pretty penny," Sammy observed. After replacing the locks on the door, Sammy mentally counted the thirteen steps back to his comfortable recliner, which was angled toward his television set. Lissy reached out to turn the television off, but Sammy stopped her.

"Naw, naw. Keep it on. I like the noise." Sammy sat down and looked straight ahead. "So, what you want from me at this hour?"

"I need some sleeping pills."

"Ever heard of the drug store? They got a whole aisle of stuff that'll knock you out."

"You know I'm not asking for ordinary stuff." Lissy paused. "I need something strong."

"What for?" Sammy pressed her.

"Sammy!" Lissy shrieked, exasperated.

"I'm your friend, Lissy," Sammy said softly. "Talk to me. Nothing can be that bad." He reached out a hand and placed it on her meaty knee.

"The less you know, the better."

"That's not gonna fly with me." Sammy sat back in his chair and folded his arms.

Lissy sighed deeply. "Sammy, did you know that in this whole big city, you're my best friend?"

Sammy didn't respond.

"I've been here for three years and an old, blind man is my best friend." Lissy cried softly. "I'm sorry if that sounds cruel."

Sammy pulled a handkerchief from his pants pocket at the same time that he released a huge burst of laughter. "What's so bad about that? Just 'cause I can't see you, don't mean I don't know what you look like." He tapped the side of his head. "I got my own picture of you right here, and it's mighty nice."

"Does that picture include a couple of breasts that could nurse a set of quadruplets on one side and triplets on the other? A pair of jugs that can turn a corner three minutes before the rest of me? Headlights that could light up a six-lane highway?"

"So you got a couple of large breasts. I got two broken eyes. So what?"

"You don't understand. People are so nasty to me because of them. I've been told my brains are in my breasts. But even with two brains, I couldn't land a decent job. And the good-looking men are the cruelest." Lissy started to cry. "My brother and sister used to call me names. Total strangers call me names. I can't take it anymore." She wiped her eyes.

"Sweetie, you think I'm spared the name-calling 'cause I can't see whose saying it." Sammy chuckled some more. "It's human nature for people to be mean and nasty to people who they think are different. You can't let 'em win, Lissy. You can't let 'em win."

"Money is not an issue." Lissy barreled forward. "I would go to this other guy I know who could help me but I'm scared I'll get caught again. I was busted once for buying drugs from an undercover cop. I don't trust myself, but I trust you."

"Oh, Lissy, baby," Sammy cooed. "I'm really sorry you been going through this. People can be so ig'nant." Sammy put a finger to his lips. "Where you get money from? You sound like you talking about real money."

"I've been saving all my tips for a breast reduction." She lowered her head. "I'm not gonna need it now."

"Lissy, you ain't talking 'bout what I think you talking 'bout?"

"I'm tired of fighting, Sammy." She gestured toward her chest, forgetting that Sammy couldn't see her. "These things have been a curse since I turned nine. I'm like the Hunchback of Notre

Dame, except I have two humps and they're in the front. I've been ostracized, persecuted and even basically accused of choosing them." Lissy took a deep breath because she could feel hysteria rising in her throat.

"For what it's worth, you beautiful to me, Lissy, and I can't even picture you as no ostrich."

Lissy smiled. Then she laughed. "Thank you, Sammy. Thank you. Only a blind man could think I'm beautiful." She wrung her hands. "Well, are you gonna help me?"

Sammy arose and went into his tiny bathroom. He came back with a prescription bottle. "I'll only give you one 'cause these things can bring down an elephant." Sammy was adamant. "And I'll only give you this one if you promise me you won't hurt yourself."

"If I promise not to hurt myself, will you give me three?" Lissy narrowed her eyes.

"Give me your hand," Sammy demanded. Lissy obeyed. He took her hand in his left hand, popped open the bottle with his right hand, and carefully poured out three pills. He didn't release her hand, however.

"You promised me," he said, his voice quivering.

Lissy leaned over to give Sammy a hug. "You have my word, Sammy. I won't hurt myself."

"Dang, girl! You ain't lyin' 'bout them Double Ds. Sure wish I could see 'em. I like big breasts!"

The next week, the hotel was hosting the Kappa Alpha Psi fraternity's annual convention. Lissy was prepared. She rarely spent any money on herself, but she had to have her special perfume. She splurged on a bit more this week, however. This week was special. This was the last week she'd allow herself to be abused. She endured the hard stares and the vulgar comments to get her hair done. She treated herself to a spa day and beauty makeover. She also purchased that one special thing that made her feel beautiful and sexy—her favorite perfume, Poison. Three ounces from Macy's cost more than a hundred dollars, but it was worth every toilet she had to scrub, every bed she had to change, every cruel remark thrown at her. She sprayed Poison on all her

The 21 Lives of Lisette Donavan   173

pulse points, including her neck and her wrists. She was most generous in that place between her breasts.

At the hotel, scores of hunky, black men in every shade of the African Diaspora roamed the hallways all day and night. They were so different—some were tall and short, some muscular and lean, others bespectacled and bearded. But they all had the same look of revulsion when they looked at Lissy. Those professional, upstanding, gorgeous guys went out of their way to kill her with unkindness.

"Hey, Myles. There's your future wife. She could nurse quads with one breast and triplets with the other."

"No, man. It's like she carrying quads *in* her breasts." They spoke in loud whispers while she walked the halls, to make sure she heard. There was no point in being cruel if she couldn't hear it. And this was before they got drunk.

"How does she stand with those things? She could put somebody's eyes out from another room."

"I'm surprised she hasn't tipped over yet."

Allen was exhausted. He could close three million dollar corporate deals until the wee hours, but he was getting too old to party until 3:00 A.M. He emptied his guts all over himself and the expensive, plush bed. When his faculties had cleared, he called the concierge and requested maid service. Such a grand and classy hotel as this, they would certainly have maids on staff who were hot. In his inebriated state, Allen perceived housekeeping was taking too long, so he stumbled to the door, opened it and saw a maid in the hallway.

"Hey, you. Get in here and clean up this room."

"My name is Lissy, sir." Lissy smiled at him. Allen was at least six-foot-two with golden-brown skin and a tight, short haircut. Although his dark eyes were bloodshot and glazed, they were still something to behold. Lissy smiled wider. He threw up at her feet.

"Whatever. Just clean up this mess." While Allen was in the bathroom, Lissy busied herself cleaning. She stripped the beds of the alcohol and vomit-soaked sheets, wiped up the disgusting remnants of Allen's dinner, and pulled out from her cleavage a small bottle containing the ground up sleeping pills. She availed herself of a bottle of Perrier from the mini-fridge and dumped half the bottle of drugs into it. She picked it up. Her humiliation would end tonight, in this room.

"You're not done, yet?" Allen demanded when he emerged from the bathroom. He was topless, his abs in grand form. Lissy couldn't stop herself from staring. Allen noticed.

"Something, huh?" he boasted. "Looks like we both have awesome chests." He laughed, and then dropped his voice to a whisper. "Except, you'll never be with this and I wouldn't touch those over your dead body."

"I know you're not feeling well, sir," Lissy said. "Perhaps, a drink of water would settle your stomach." Lissy offered him the glass. He eyed her suspiciously and then took the glass from her. He downed it in one gulp.

"God, that was bitter," Allen complained. "What was that?"

"Perrier, sir," Lissy explained.

Lissy watched as Allen became drowsier and drowsier. He could barely keep his eyes open. Lissy began to unbutton her uniform top. She peeled it off and let it drop to the floor.

"What are you doing?" Allen asked, his words slurred. He fell back on the bed, incapacitated.

Lissy next removed her bra and emancipated her ample breasts. She walked slowly toward the bed, toward Allen. She lifted his handsome head and brought it to that warm, soft spot between her breasts. For a full three minutes, she applied pressure to the back of his head, making sure his nose was deep in the folds of her flesh. He struggled slightly for a little while, and then he stopped. When Lissy released him, he flopped back onto the bed, lifeless.

"Not over my dead body, sir," Lissy said to herself. "Over yours."

The New York City detective who was called in to process the crime scene was baffled. Another perfectly healthy, successful, young black man.

"That's the sixth one this month, not counting the three during the Kappa Alpha Psi convention," he complained to the female forensic photographer. "They're all from different states, went to different schools, worked for different companies. We've got a serial killer in this hotel, and I can't figure out what these guys have in common."

"I'll tell you what," she responded between frames. "It's a shame. All these guys were gorgeous."

The detective sniffed the air. "Do you smell that? I could swear I've smelled that smell before. It's strongest around the victim's head." He got closer to the dead man's face.

"They were all drugged, then asphyxiated, but with what?"

The female photographer put her camera down and sniffed around the dead man. "I know that scent. It's Poison. That means a woman. Probably educated and rich."

The door to room opened suddenly. "Excuse me, sir. Will you be needing anything from housekeeping?"

The detective took a mental note of the woman's gigantic, bodacious headlights. He was a breast man himself. Then, he turned back to the dead man.

"No, nothing yet." He walked over to the door and closed it as Lissy backed out of the room with her cart.

"There's that scent again."

20. Double D Death, Felicia S.W. Thomas,
    feliciathomas917@hotmail.com

21.

You Don't Even Know My Name

Barbara Joe Williams

"*Lisette* Anita Donavan, will you marry me?"

The most handsome man I'd ever met was on bended knee asking the one question I'd longed to hear all of my twenty-eight years on earth.

Gregory Lamar continued. "I love you, Lissy, and I want you for my bride. Please, say you'll marry me."

My eyes wandered around the dimly-lit Chinese restaurant and just like I'd figured, all eyes were on us. While swallowing the last savory bite of shrimp fried rice, my heart skipped several beats as I held my breath. How could I say no to the man I loved? How could I embarrass him in front of all these people? How would I ever tell him that my real name wasn't even Lisette?

"Yes, I'll marry you," I replied, releasing a long-held breath. Praying against all prayers that this relationship would somehow work out, I knew I'd have to come clean someday about my criminal past, but today wasn't going to be the day.

Everyone in the place clapped for joy as Gregory slipped the two-carat, bling ring on my finger. With his muscled arms wrapped around me, I felt secure in his embrace. He spent three days a week working out at the gym, and it was truly paying off. I couldn't have dreamt of a finer mate if I'd picked him out of a new age fashion catalog. As much as he reminded me of the dark chocolate model and soul singer, Tyrese, he was much better than that. We were a perfect fit in bed and out. I was just a few inches shorter than his six-foot frame. Although I didn't work out as often as he did, I kept in shape by walking to the Grand Hotel, across from Central Park, where I worked five days a week.

For the last six months, Greg had treated me like a Nubian princess and now he wanted to make me his queen. I returned his hug with all the joy in my body. I'd never meant to deceive him, but I had been doing just that from the first day we'd met. Since I'm living life on the run, what choice did I have? Did I mean for it to go this far? No, I didn't. Could I have stopped us from becoming this close? Yes, I could have. But Gregory Lamar was the epitome of maleness. And on top of that, he was the kindest and gentlest man I'd met in years. I couldn't let my past indiscretions ruin my future happiness. Would you?

I felt the anxiety creeping through my bones like a cold chill on a wintery day. Still, I fought to keep my voice calm. "Excuse me, darling. I have to run to the ladies room before we leave," I said, clutching my purse.

Greg stood up, kissed me on the lips, and said, "Hurry back. I don't want you out of my sight any longer than necessary."

I rushed into the freshly cleaned restroom, splashed cold water on my face, and stared at my reflection in the gleaming mirror. I saw caramel skin and deep set brown eyes staring back at me. My full lips kept telling me that this wasn't a good time to be having another panic attack, not after all I'd been through to make my way from Bossier City to the heart of New York City. Reaching into my evening bag, I pulled out my Fashion Fair bronze lip gloss and freshened up my soup coolers. After taking several deep breaths and focusing on my new rock, I strolled back to my dinner table with a seemingly level head.

As we walked out of the five-star restaurant hand in hand, my heart continued fluttering with joy. Simultaneously, my stomach ached from nervousness. My feet were throbbing from working all day as a maid, a job I hated but was lucky to have. There wasn't much I could do in the Big Apple, especially since my bachelor's degree in technology was in my birth name, Denise Johnson.

Greg pulled out my chair. I'd just slipped into my seat when he asked, "Are you okay? I mean you're happy, right?" He was looking down at me with a hint of worry in his handsome eyes. A face like his was meant to be captured in pictures.

Pasting on my best smile, I replied, "Yes, I've never been happier in my life." Those were the words that crossed my lips, but many questions crossed my heart. I was wondering how he would react to my confession. Would he leave me like a baby orphan crying at his feet? Or would he stay and hold me through the night like a loving teddy bear? Either way, I was determined to make this a special evening for both of us and let the future take care of itself.

On the drive to his apartment, my mind was all over the place. Greg made a great living working in his father's business as a cleaning supplies salesman. That's how we met—on the job. He walked into the building carrying cases of sample products. I couldn't stop staring at his bulging biceps until my co-worker, Kandi, tapped me on the shoulder and said, "Don't you know it's not polite to stare at strangers? Even if they are as f-i-n-e as they come." And we both laughed like teenagers at a Valentine's Day dance.

At the age of thirty, Greg had a high-rise apartment, a new Mercedes, and to top it all off, he had never been married nor had any children, just like me. We both had one older brother and a younger sister, which made us middle children. We also shared a desire to own our own businesses someday and fulfill the American Dream. It appeared as if we had much in common on the outside. Only I knew something that Greg didn't know. He'd fallen in love with an escaped convict, who'd fallen in love with the wrong man just two years prior to meeting him.

Nothing in my life had ever come close to being this bittersweet. As special as I felt at that moment, being a newly engaged woman, I could have shot myself for loving Raymond Scott for five years, for letting him talk me into driving a getaway car for him after he and his dumb friend, Anthony Holmes, decided to rob the First National Bank in Bossier City, Louisiana. I was crazy enough to think that I wouldn't be convicted because I was under the influence of love, which is stronger than 80 proof alcohol or heroin, and I was only the driver. But when the judge brought that gravel down declaring that I spend the next ten years of my life in prison, I had to find a way to escape.

Just like in the movies, I pretended to use the bathroom, and crawled out of the small window at the back of the courthouse. I really didn't think that it would work, but I was blessed to be a size two, and slipped through the narrow opening easier than melted butter. And since I'd won several medals for running track in high school, I hit the ground faster than an Olympic champion, and never looked back.

"Baby, baby, we're here," Greg whispered. I raised my head, surprised that I'd drifted off to sleep on the ride to his apartment. "Wake up. I hope you enjoyed your nap, because we're going to be up for hours." He gave me that sexy smile, the one that always gave me more goose bumps than the telephone ringing at midnight. Just my luck, "You Don't Even Know My Name" by Alicia Keys was playing on the radio and Greg was humming along with the smooth melody. It was at the bridge part and she was asking the guy, "Can you hear me now?" I wanted to dissolve into the leather seats as Greg jumped out the car and came around to open my door.

It was after ten o'clock when I entered his uptown apartment. I was half asleep until he opened the front door, stepped aside, and said, "Welcome to your future home." He clapped his hands one time, and slow music filled the room. I rubbed my tired eyes, kicked off my four-inch pumps, and pumped myself up. My widened eyes and bare feet followed the trail of fresh, red rose petals leading all the way into the master suite and into the master bathroom. More rose petals were in the oversized Jacuzzi flowing with a full-drawn bath. Red candles burned around the rim of the tub, giving the room a soft, warming glow and a heavenly smell.

I turned to look at Greg, and asked, "How? I mean—when did you do all this? We've been at the restaurant for hours."

He laughed at my bewildered expression. It wasn't often that he got to surprise me because I made it clear early on in our relationship that I didn't like surprises. "Well, while you were in the ladies room, I texted my sister and had her set this all up for me. You like?" he asked, stretching out his arms.

I snapped back, "Yes, I love it. Remind me to thank Val."

Sitting down on the side of the tub, I lowered my hand into the water, and enjoyed the warmness swirling around my fingers. The water was the perfect temperature for bathing and relaxing together. When I turned back to look up at Greg, he'd already removed his shirt, and was creeping towards me. I inhaled his masculine scent and prayed that this moment, this night, and this life would last forever.

"Lisette Anita Donavan, will you marry me?" That's all I kept hearing during the restless night that I'd had. And all I could think about was that it wasn't even my real name. I knew it wouldn't be right for me to enter a marriage agreement under those circumstances. Maybe I wasn't the most moral person in the world, but I had to ask myself the question: Would I want him to tell me if the situation was reversed? And the answer was a resounding yes. I couldn't risk marrying him, starting a family, and then five years from now having my picture pop up on "America's Most Wanted" or some other show highlighting fugitives.

No, I couldn't go out like that. But I didn't want to lose the only solid thing in my life. It was already hard enough being isolated from my family and old friends. The only people I knew in New York were a few co-workers and Greg. Whenever he asked me about my past life, I told him that I was a free-spirit, disconnected from family, and looking for a fortune in the big city. I mean, what better place to blend in than this?

"What's wrong, baby? Is something bothering you?" Greg asked, staring at me with those droopy bedroom eyes. With one arm covering my bosom, he gently kissed the base of my neck. "You know, if you don't like the ring, we can take it back together and get—"

"No, Greg!" That was it. I had to stop him right there. I didn't know which was pounding harder, my head or my heart, but I told them both to be still long enough for me to get the truth out. Slipping from under the satiny sheets, I walked around the room trying to gather up my clothes. For whatever reason, I didn't want to have this conversation in the nude. My soul burned from the thought of hurting this man who only wanted to love me and show me a better life. I'd never forgive myself for losing someone as wonderful as he was.

Greg stared at me like I was transforming into an alien being from Mars. I couldn't begin to imagine the thoughts that were going through his mind. He was sitting up in bed with the sheet draped over his pelvis—the area that I was going to miss more than crispy bacon for breakfast. "Lissy, whatever it is, just say it."

"I really want to marry you, Greg. But there are things about my past that you need to know."

"Like what?" he asked.

"You don't even know my name. It's not Lissy, it's Denise." His eyes met mine, and I saw his expression change from compassion to confusion. I crept over to his side of the bed, eased down beside him, and let my tears flow like the Nile River. In between my sobs, I managed to tell him how I'd fallen for a lowlife married man in Bossier City who almost cost me years in prison. I didn't expect him to forgive me right away, but I didn't expect what came next either.

Greg bolted from the bed stark naked, ran into the bathroom, and locked the door. I held my breath waiting for his return. Eventually, I had to breathe because it didn't seem like he was coming out any time soon. I tipped over to the door, listening for some sign of life in the other room. What I heard was him sobbing worse than a newborn baby who hadn't eaten in six hours and whose throat had gotten sore from screaming. My heart shattered into more pieces than I'd ever be able to count, even if I lived to be ninety-nine years old.

Minutes passed before Greg emerged from the bathroom with a towel wrapped around his waist. He didn't speak to me or look at me as he headed to the dresser, pulled out a pair of underpants, pulled on a pair of distressed jeans, slipped on a white t-shirt, and rammed his feet into a pair of Nike sneakers. I was just sitting there, waiting for him to say something, to curse me out, or slap me; wishing he'd take some action, even if it was violent.

Well, I got my wish because the next thing he did was grab his car keys, turn to me, and say, "I'm going out for an hour. And when I return, I want you and all your stuff gone. I don't ever want to see you again. Do you understand me?" He spoke in a slow, methodical tone, letting me know that he was serious.

My heart told me to beg for his forgiveness, wrap my arms around those biceps that I loved so much, and plead for mercy like I'd done in the Louisiana court. Then, my mind begged me to be quiet. I listened to my mind. Why? Because I knew that I didn't deserve him. He was too good for me anyway. Who was I to ruin his perfect life? Who was I fooling by thinking that I was fooling him when I was only fooling myself? I sat there in silence and watched my greatest love leave me dissipating into tears. My whole being became a living puddle.

Eventually, the water dried up. My body was weak but strong enough to gather up the few things I'd left at his house: a nightgown, one maid's uniform, a jogging suit, a pair of loafers, and some toiletries. I checked my cell phone and realized that my hour was almost up. I didn't want to be there when he returned, especially since I didn't have a clue about what was going through his mind or how he'd react to me still being there.

After I got cleaned up and stuffed by belongings into a small overnight case, I headed for the front door. Abruptly, I stopped and turned around. I wanted just one more picture of what I could have had embedded in my brains before walking outside into a new life again. When I turned back towards the exit, Greg was blocking my way, and clutching the doorknob. My heart went crazy, beating louder than a freight train whistle blowing in my ear. I couldn't move or speak. I was frozen tighter than an ice pack.

My blurry eyes focused on his swollen ones. He stepped into the living room, closed the door behind him, and spoke words that shocked me to the core. "It's okay, Denise. You don't even know my name, either. I'm not really Gregory Lamar."

21. You Don't Even Know My Name, Barbara Joe Williams, amanipublishing@aol.com

Contributing Authors Contact List

In order for us to keep growing as writers, you're encouraged to provide specific feedback to individual authors at this time via email:

1. Full Circle, Shantae Charles, shantaecharles333@gmail.com

2. A Wicked Twist of Fate, Angela Y. Hodge, angelayhodge@gmail.com

3. There Are No Mountains, John McPhaul, xuannam66@embarqmail.com

4. Empty Pockets, Laurina Osborne, laurinao@yahoo.com

5. You Can Never Leave, Melinda Michelle, gwendolynevans21@yahoo.com

6. Last Date with Elijah, Thomas R. Wilson, TallahasseeWriter@yahoo.com

7. My Happy, Xavier D. Woods, southwood3716-2@comcast.net

8. Wrong Turns, Irma Clark, ineclark@cs.com

9. Country Girl, City Girl, Bad Girl, Jane Ann Keil-Stevens, jast820@comcast.net

10. Family Ties, Shay Shoats, KBShoats@gmail.com

11. A Voice of MY Own, Anita L. Gray, neeterlrg@gmail.com

12. In Due Time, Erica Belcher, enbelcher@yahoo.com

13. Accomplice, Sylvia Livingston,
    Sylvia.Livingston@yahoo.com

14. I Want My Piece, Tremayne Moore,
    tremayne_moore@yahoo.com

15. Maid to Survive, Karen Randolph, Randolphkd@aol.com

16. Lissy Transforming, Angelia Vernon Menchan,
    acvermen@yahoo.com

17. Lisette Donavan's American Dream, Cheryl B.Williams,
    clbwms@gmail.com

18. Diary of a Sneaky Woman, Michael Beckford,
    michaelbeckford@gmail.com
19. The Snake: Kenneth E. Taite, kennethtaite@gmail.com

20. Double D Death, Felicia S.W. Thomas,
    feliciathomas917@hotmail.com

21. You Don't Even Know My Name, Barbara Joe Williams,
    amanipublishing@aol.com

Thank you for reading our stories. If you don't mind, please take a few minutes to vote for your favorite story and author by visiting this site:

www.surveybuilder.com/s/libae_keiaa

You may also contact the publisher via email at:

amanipublishing@aol.com

Or visit her website at:

www.barbarajoewilliams.com

Join the Tallahassee Authors Network on Facebook at:

www.facebook.com

Tallahassee
AUTHORS
Network

CPSIA information can be obtained at www.ICGtesting.com
Printed in the USA
LVOW041518250512

283341LV00005B/88/P